P9-DXN-710

The HOUSE of Serendipity

LUCY IVISON

ILLUSTRATED BY LUCY TRUMAN

WITHDRAWN

RAZORBILL

RAZORBILL

An imprint of Penguin Random House LLC, New York

First published in the United Kingdom by Usborne Publishing Ltd., 2021
Published in the United States of America by Razorbill,
an imprint of Penguin Random House LLC, 2021

Text copyright © 2021 by Lucy Ivison
Illustrations copyright © 2021 by Lucy Truman

Penguin supports copyright. Copyright fuels creativity, encourages diverse voices, promotes free speech, and creates a vibrant culture. Thank you for buying an authorized edition of this book and for complying with copyright laws by not reproducing, scanning, or distributing any part of it in any form without permission. You are supporting writers and allowing Penguin to continue to publish books for every reader.

Razorbill & colophon are registered trademarks of Penguin Random House LLC.

Visit us online at penguinrandomhouse.com.

LIBRARY OF CONGRESS CATALOGING-IN-PUBLICATION DATA
Names: Ivison, Lucy, author. | Truman, Lucy, illustrator.
Title: The House of Serendipity / Lucy Ivison ; illustrated by Lucy Truman.
Description: New York : Razorbill, [2021] | Audience: Ages 8–12.
Summary: At Serendipity House, a grand mansion in 1920s London, two girls, one living downstairs as a servant and the other living in wealth upstairs, combine their fashion designing and dressmaking talents to secretly make outfits for the debutante ball and help one attendee who wants to escape high-society life.
Identifiers: LCCN 2021000999 | ISBN 9780593204726 (hardcover)
ISBN 9780593204740 (trade paperback) | ISBN 9780593204733 (ebook)
Subjects: CYAC: Dressmaking—Fiction. | Fashion design—Fiction.
Social classes—Fiction. | Friendship—Fiction. | London (England)—History—
20th century—Fiction. | Great Britain—History—George V, 1910–1936—Fiction.
Classification: LCC PZ7.1.I985 Ho 2021 | DDC [Fic]—dc23
LC record available at https://lccn.loc.gov/2021000999

Manufactured in Italy

1 3 5 7 9 10 8 6 4 2

Design by Rebecca Aidlin
Text set in Excelsior LT Std

This is a work of historical fiction. Apart from the well-known actual people, events, and locales that figure in the narrative, all names, characters, places, and incidents are the products of the author's imagination or are used fictitiously. Any resemblance to current events or locales, or to living persons, is entirely coincidental.

The publisher does not have any control over and does not assume any responsibility for author or third-party websites or their content.

For my mother, Rosie,
who brought me up in a house full of
magic, imagination, and vintage clothes.
Who, like Sylvia, sees every new outfit as
an opportunity for reinvention.

And for my auntie Annabel,
whose superpower is dressmaking.
Whether it was a Maid Marian costume
or a Gucci suit, you have always made
my fashion dreams come true.
Myrtle is for you.

1

THE FIRST CUT IN THE PATTERN

Myrtle

I stopped and set my sewing machine down for the hundredth time. My hand was red raw, and my whole body ached with the effort of carrying the machine across London. But I refused to leave it behind.

I caught my reflection in the shop window and smiled to myself. Ma had said this dress was my best work, and it was. *I* had designed it and stayed up all night making it. If I were going to be a maid, I had decided I would do it dressed as though I were a queen.

I based the dress on a design from Chanel's last winter collection. All the magazines featured it, and every day another lady would come into our family tailor's shop, grasping a clipping, wanting it copied, desperate to look as chic and beautiful as the picture. But my dress is only Chanel-inspired. The rest is Myrtle Mathers. Instead of cutting it out of navy crepe, I used the finest black wool, soft but strong. I changed the collar so it is wider and gently scalloped, and I trimmed it in silk. On the tips I embroidered the tiniest bumblebees, the symbol of the worker. The Chanel dress had wide sleeves that flared out at the cuff, but I designed mine so the cuffs are tight to my wrists and won't drag in soapy water or ashes in the hearth. I sewed on tiny black pearl buttons that reach all the way from my wrists to my elbows, and then I fluted the hem so that when I walk it swishes ever so slightly. And if you pay attention as it swishes, you will catch glimpses of the life I am leaving behind.

Because along the hem I embroidered a paw print the exact shape and size of our cat's, Schiaparelli. I stitched my mother's favorite forget-me-not teacup and my father's lucky scissors. There are two braids, one for me and one for my neighbor Ethel, tied together with our matching best-friend ribbons. In a delicate chain stitch is our door with its number 7, old cracked paving stones in front, and the year, 1926. I stitched a cinema ticket and a Victoria sponge cake, my copy of *Peter Pan* and a reel of cotton.

I picked up my suitcase and sewing machine again and started to walk. With every step I was walking farther away from my *before* life. My life with a ma and pa. A life spent making things together in our tailor's shop. A life where I be-lieved I would become a dressmaker like them one day.

The most important cut in a pattern is the first one. It is irreversible. My life *before* was like a huge piece of uncut fab-ric. Pa dying was the first cut in my pattern. Ma got sick too, but then she got better. Well, almost better. But then she had to sell our shop to pay our debts—another snip—and go back

cinema

OLYMPIA THEATRE
LONDON
SEAT 42   ADMIT ONE   TOTAL 2 1   146272

embroidered collar

Myrtle

Braided Swirls
(chain stitch)

CINEMA

PETER PAN

The door

embroider
the cracked paving

1920

TeaCup

Cotton

to Ireland, to the farm and to my nana, where the air is fresh and her lungs can fully heal. Saying goodbye to her, and not knowing when I would see her again, was a slash across the very seams of me. But I stayed in London because there are more jobs here for girls like me. More opportunities to become what you want to be. And I want to be someone. Someone who can bring my mother home. Someone who won't let go of my dreams. Coco Chanel left her orphanage with just her scissors, and now I am leaving Stepney with my sewing machine. I am alone, cutting my own pattern, making my own life.

The street opened onto an impossibly grand square. There were four mansions, but I knew instantly which one was Serendipity House. It shone brilliantly white in the spring sunshine and, from a distance, seemed to be encased in its own private snowstorm. I squinted and realized what appeared to be snow was actually thousands and thousands of tiny pink cherry blossom petals swirling in the wind. Something in my heart lifted. The main door was vast, and a woman in an old-fashioned wool suit holding a carpet bag stood in front of it. I saw the sign for the servants' entrance and looked back across the square to where I had come from, back toward home. And then I looked up at the pink blizzard, closed my eyes, and stepped into it.

2

A LEMON GROVE APPEARS
IN THE SCHOOLROOM

Sylvia

I heard the clang of the doorbell and picked up momentum as I raced down the stairs. Miss Smurfett, my governess, had arrived at the perfect moment to witness the dazzling effect of my cloak. As I leaped, it splayed out dramatically, as planned, and I landed at her feet with a flourish.

Miss Smurfett is like a large barn owl: mostly, it is only her eyes that move. She had little reaction to my entrance. She calmly dusted some cherry blossoms off her jacket and said, "I see you are back in daywear, Lady Sylvia."

I like to dress to suit my daydreams. Last week after reading *Jane Eyre* I spent every day in Grandmama's nightdress, but I am over that phase now. This week I am simply squiffy for *The Three Musketeers*. I have painted tiny moons and stars around my eyes and filled my hair with silk flowers in different shades of sunset to offset the scarlet cloak I found in the attic. So far, I have found that everything feels more conspiratorial and urgent if you say it while swooshing your cloak.

I tried it out on the Smurf. "Come to the schoolroom, we are under siege."

We wound our way up the stairs to the part of the house only Smurf and I usually frequent. I flung the door to the schoolroom open. "Can you believe it? We have been bamboozled. And *just* when I was *so* adoring all of those triangles."

Miss Smurfett raised an eyebrow. "Pythagoras is indeed fascinating."

We both surveyed the usually dull and tired room. It was tired and dull no more, because my stepmother, Marmalade, had gone fully bananas preparing for my sister Delphine's debutante ball. Since the previous day, dozens and dozens of lemon trees in wooden pots painted silver and gold had appeared and now completely filled the room.

"They arrived from Italy this morning. You know two hundred and fifty people are invited? How do you like that? Two hundred and fifty people coming to a ball in my own house, and I'm not allowed to go!" I slumped down next to a lemon tree. "Poor show is what I call it. Haven't I been telling you for the longest time, Smurf, that Delphine has become the most fearful traitor? Imagine not inviting your own sister to your ball!"

Miss Smurfett lowered herself gingerly onto the edge of the lemon tree pot next to mine and fixed her twinkling eyes on me. "Lady Sylvia. Even if Lady Delphine wanted to invite you, she couldn't. You are not out in society yet, it's not allowed. You are just a little too young for balls."

"Too young to do anything except be trapped in this

house! Smurf, you know you are my only friend now? Too, too dreadful when your governess is your only friend, wouldn't you say? No offense intended and all that."

Miss Smurfett nodded one of her slow nods.

"Delphine *used* to be fun. Do you remember when she would chase us and pretend to be a carrot possessed by the devil? Now all she cares about is embroidering handkerchiefs and dance cards and who she's going to marry. She barely talks to me anymore. Which is fine by me because she has become such a terrible bore!" I kicked my pot hard and a lemon fell into my lap.

Miss Smurfett reached across and put her hand on my arm. "I am sorry, Lady Sylvia. I know how dearly girls your age crave chums."

It stung that even Smurf felt bad for me, so I let myself pout a bit. But then I had a flash of inspiration. Why pout about the place when there are tricks to be found? I am not a girl to let a moment slip. One of the reasons I consider Miss Smurfett a comrade in arms and friend more than a governess is that she really has very little interest in education, which is very much exactly the same as me. We spend most of our time supposing things and going to the zoo. Miss Smurfett was my stepmother's governess, and Marmalade considers her to have done an excellent job at not discombobulating her mind with too many facts. She says it is impossible to focus with too much information washing around up there and that Miss Smurfett understands that entirely.

I tried to sound authoritative and spontaneous. "Anyway." I sighed dramatically. "There is simply no point trying to do any type of schoolwork today. Honestly, I would love to get back among the equations, but there isn't a room free in the house. Even Father's study is full of gold eggs."

I slipped my arm through the Smurf's. "The most selfless thing we can do is go out . . . to the theater?"

Miss Smurfett's eyes lit up immediately. The Smurf loves the theater even more than the zoo.

"*Macbeth*," she said with a quiver.

"With tea at the Ritz first. We mustn't go hungry."

Miss Smurfett tried to sound offhand. "Shall you be . . . dressing for the theater?"

I twirled and took off back down the stairs. "I should think I am very much dressed for the theater already," I shouted back up at her. "I look extremely theatrical."

3

BELOWSTAIRS

Myrtle

All the way across London I had imagined knocking on a huge grand door and it being opened to dozens of people all staring at me. I had practiced again and again the exact way I would say my name, slowly and surely with my head held high. But in the end the servants' door was wide open and I just stood, covered in pink petals, gawking, waiting for someone to notice me.

The kitchen was full. Three girls, older than me, were cutting pastry into stars, and a tiny shrewlike woman, who was obviously the cook, was stirring the biggest pot of custard I had ever seen. People kept coming in and out, picking up trays and jars and tea towels. I started to feel ridiculous. What if no one noticed I was here at all and I had to stand all night, growing pinker and pinker with petals and embarrassment, my suitcase in my hand, just waiting to be seen?

A girl with very white-blonde hair swapped her star cutter for a moon one. "Well, I like Lady Delphine, and I feel sorry for her. Poor lamb, she's been crying up there about her dress for an hour. Do you remember when Trixie's mother made her get married in her cousin's frock? She looked like a prize pig. The pink was the exact same shade as her face."

The other two giggled. "Yes, but Trixie had no money," one said, "and only ten people at her wedding. I thought they went all the way to Paris to get Lady Delphine's ball dress. I mean, has anyone actually *seen* it?"

"I wish we could sneak up and have a gander," the third said.

"There'll be none of that," the cook said sternly without turning around.

"There's all this commotion, and we're all working like dogs, and is this ball even going to happen? That's what I want to know," said a girl with tightly curled hair spilling out of a braid.

The oldest of the three girls snorted. "Don't be daft. The queen and Princess Mary are attending. What do you think they're going to do? Shut the door in their faces because the dress isn't right?"

"It must be rotten having such a knockout beauty like the duchess as a stepmother. I mean, you want everyone looking at *you* at your coming-out ball," the white-blonde girl said with a sigh.

"Well, when you get presented to the queen, Dot, and we have to make you seventeen thousand gold stars to hang from the ceiling and twenty-five trifles, we'll be sure we're all lookin' at you."

As they burst out laughing, the shrew-cook whipped round. "That is enough! As if we don't have enough to do without you three turning into music hall acts. I want silence in this kitch—"And then she saw me.

I took a deep breath and gripped the handle of my suitcase. "I'm Myrtle Mathers." I said it too quickly, before anyone had asked. The three girls all turned and looked at me. "The new maid."

The cook nodded curtly. "You just left your mother?"

For a moment I thought about how dark and flat my mother's eyes had gone as we said goodbye. How long and hard she had hugged me and how I could feel what we were both losing as we were losing it. I thought about the brown package she had pressed into my hands and how she hadn't looked back at me, and how I had known why. I straightened my back and nodded at the cook. I made my voice come out clear and strong. "Yes. She's gone back to Ireland. My father died of tuberculosis last month and she hadn't the money to keep both me and her, so she's gone home and I am . . ."

The cook looked right at me for a second as if she could see exactly what was playing in my mind. "And now you're with us, lovey."

The girls all smiled at me as if to say they were sorry. Cook pointed her spoon at the girl with white-blonde hair. "That's Dot, who is our resident smarty-pants." Then she aimed her spoon at the girl with braid. "That's Mary, and over there ruining my shortbread is Gladys." Gladys smiled at me over her thick-rimmed glasses. "Dot will get you a cup of tea, and then she can show you to your room. You can have a sit-down and unpack your things, and then we'll introduce you to the duchess and give you a tour of the house."

"I don't need a rest just now," I said. "I can see you're busy, and I don't mind helping."

"*Busy* ain't even the word, Myrtle," Dot said. "We don't even know what day of the week it is down 'ere anymore."

They laughed, and I put my things down in the corner, took off my coat and hat and hung them by the door, found an apron, and picked up a star cutter. The cook turned back to the custard and everything carried on, except with me there, in a very strange place, with people I had never met before, but who I would be living with from now on.

"Well, you've come just as it's *all* going on," Dot whispered. "Do you know what a coming-out is?"

"Sort of. I know from all the magazines that there is a *season,* and that if you are doing it, you need clothes to go to the races at Ascot, and a special white dress for when you are presented at the palace, and then lots of suits and dresses for luncheons and things."

Gladys snorted. "If *you* are doing it? Ain't none of us gonna be up at that palace. But blooming 'eck, Myrtle, you know more than I did. I had never heard of it before everyone started going on about Lady Delphine's *coming-out.* I was like, *Where's she coming out of? Prison?*"

Everyone laughed and I started to feel a tiny bit more relaxed. I kept cutting stars out and sneaking glances at the girls.

Dot seemed the most confident. "Lady Delphine went to the palace to be presented last week, with the duke and duchess, of course. We all lined up as she left."

The way the girls were with each other was so easy, as if they were sisters. It made me feel relaxed too. "So, what happens next?"

Dot grinned. "Well, all the girls who got presented need to get married, so every single one has a grand ball, and it's just a big ol' race to get the debs' delights."

"Like an egg and spoon but with lots of diamonds and trifles thrown in." Gladys giggled.

"Debs' delights?" I couldn't help but get swept up in it, and Dot and Gladys were falling over themselves to be the ones to tell all.

"They are the fellas who have all the money and the grand houses—" Dot started.

"—and then by Christmas, everyone is in love and engaged. Ta-da!" Gladys couldn't help herself.

It didn't seem strange the way they spoke about it. As if they were just explaining how lions live in Africa or the way some spiders eat their mates. It was just how another species did it.

"What happens to you if you don't fall in love and get engaged?"

"What happens if you don't get engaged?" Dot shouted to no one in particular.

"You turn into a pumpkin," Cook shouted back. "And then we have to do this whole bleedin' ball again next year, so let's hope this dress gets sorted and everyone who wants to get married does. Only then I'll have a whole wedding to cater for."

"Why does she hate her dress so much?" I asked Dot.

"Well," Dot whispered, "none of us know. She won't come out of her room."

And then the most beautiful person I have seen in real life swept into the kitchen. She had incredibly long auburn hair that was loose except for a bright turquoise scarf wound through it. She was wearing a cream silk blouse with a mandarin collar and loose cuffs and a cream wool skirt that finished just above her ankles so you could see her white stockings. I know ladies wear silver and gold kid leather shoes for dancing, but I had never seen a pair. And I had definitely never seen brightly colored shoes before. This lady's were the exact same turquoise as her scarf, with a T-bar across the front. She didn't look very old. Thirty, maybe. I wondered if she was Lady Delphine.

Dot, Gladys, and Mary all stood up, so I did too.

The lady looked at me. "Who is this extremely solemn-looking thing?"

"I'm Myrtle Mathers." This time it came out a bit more like I had practiced, and I curtsied the way Ma had shown me, not too deep but with my head bowed.

"Of course you are. Thank *goodness* you are here." She winked at me. "This whole thing is of course my fault because I *adore* parties. And as you probably know, the queen hates me, so I am going to show her a thing or two about how to throw a ball. Hers are always so *expected*. And what do we all want from life if not the *unexpected*?"

Nobody responded. Cook shuffled as if she were searching for an appropriate response.

"Don't be fooled, girls. Everyone thinks she hates me because I was called the beauty of the age in *The Tatler*. But that is not why. Being famous for being beautiful is gauche, as you well know." Again, no response from anyone in the kitchen. "No one knew what lilac *was* until I wore it, and she *detests* that."

She picked up a spoon from the table, walked over to the pot of custard, and scooped some out. "I simply live for custard. Too, too divine." She put the spoon in her mouth. I had never seen a woman as bold as her. She was bold as brass and then some. I couldn't believe it. The women I grew up with care about having the right hat for church and making sure your doorstep shines so no one can say you are not *respectable*. They want people to think they are *ladylike*. But this actual lady didn't seem to care. Being near her felt thrilling, as if anything could happen next.

"We need to treat this like the war," she continued. "Only three days to go! All hands on deck and we *shall* overcome. This ball is going to be the most scandalous ball on record, even if I have to strip naked and dance the tango with the king himself."

Dot giggled and Cook looked quite aghast. Part of me couldn't believe I was standing opposite someone who *knew* the king of England and was mentioning unmentionable things in the same sentence as him, but then seeing how beautiful and elegant and daring she was, I instantly knew it was all true too.

"Balls are a serious business, Dot." And then the lady did a double take and her dancing smile rested on me. "What an *incredibly* smart dress, Myrtle Mathers." She looked me up and down. "Is this standard issue now, Cook? Coco Chanel for the maids?"

My heart swelled with the compliment. A real aristocratic lady noticing my handiwork. "I made it," I said. "I can dress-make, ma'am."

The lady smiled. "You certainly can. How very delicious of you. It is *quite* the thing. You don't do a line in Parisian haute couture ball gowns, do you?" And then she let out peals of laughter. "Oh, darling Cook, I only came to sort of pretend to check on all the preparations, and it all looks jolly industrious, I must say. Bravo, bravo, especially for the custard." And then she floated out.

"Well, that was the duchess," Cook said matter-of-factly.

And the working hum of the kitchen resumed. As I rolled out the pastry, I looked up at the rows and rows of tiny bells arranged on the wall opposite me. They were all labeled in neat gold lettering: *The Drawing Room, The Duke's Study, The Duchess's Dressing Room, The Garden Room, Lady Delphine's Room*, and then a name I hadn't heard mentioned: *Lady Sylvia's Room.*

"Does Lady Delphine have a sister?" I asked politely.

Dot's face split into a huge grin, and Mary and Gladys giggled. Even Cook smiled to herself as she stirred the custard.

"What?" I said. "What's she like?"

Dot shook her head. "Lady Sylvia is . . ."

Gladys opened her mouth and closed it again.

"She's . . ." Mary trailed off.

Cook glanced up at me. "There's no describing Lady Sylvia, Myrtle. I mean, the duchess is unusual to be sure, but they broke the mold with Lady Sylvia. She's . . . Well, you'll just have to see for yourself."

4

MIDNIGHT IN VENICE

Sylvia

As soon as I had gathered my sketchbook and huge yellow umbrella, the Smurf and I set out. I launched headfirst, loudly and without stopping, into the minute details of the ball. Smurf finds such things captivating, and I knew it would prevent her from having one of her misguided educational outbursts. The type where she starts spouting off the Latin names for plants or telling me what some or other Romantic poet thought about Shakespeare, in some odd notion that it will be useful to my life.

I looped my arm through hers. "Did you know the ball has a theme? It's all the rage now." I rolled my eyes. "Apparently, you're simply no one in the season if your ball *doesn't* have a theme."

"Really? How novel. And what is the theme, I wonder, with all those lemon trees? Citrus Fruits of the Continent?"

I snorted. "It's not a geography textbook, Smurf. Good thing governesses don't invent the themes. Imagine . . . 'You are invited to celebrate an algebra-filled night of decadence at the palace.'"

"Indeed, Lady Sylvia. The educated in charge of decisions, perish the thought!"

"Midnight in Venice," I said melodramatically, and feigned a swoon. "It's a masquerade ball. There are circus performers and orange jelly and a replica of the opera house made entirely from sugared almonds. Honestly, it's the *least* Delphine thing ever to have happened."

"Did she want a different theme? Midday in the Cotswolds, perhaps?" Miss Smurfett's eyes twinkled.

"Three p.m. in the Lavatory." I burst into loud giggles and definitely saw Smurf suppress a smile. "Honestly, everyone has gone completely mad about it. I'm not allowed to roam freely about my own house. It's not just the lemon grove, you know, Smurf? There are decorations *everywhere*. Even the stables are full of enormous pretend lily pads they are going to hang from the ceiling of the summer house. I should think the horses are most confused. And Cook found three hundred Venetian masks in the cold larder, which is why there was no cream with tea yesterday. Marmalade is really going batty for it. She wants it to be the *ball of the century*. Which is all very well, but we didn't even have proper breakfast—we had to have a sort of army picnic. Father said he felt like he was back at the front."

"Well, your turn will come. When it is *your* debutante ball, I'm sure everyone will make sacrifices."

"Gosh, Smurf, I shan't be having one. I've made a solemn vow not to get married, you know, like a nun. I mean, I won't actually become a nun—"

"No, Lady Sylvia."

"Such boring outfits, and you have to get up frightfully early *and* dedicate your life to God. I haven't worked out what to dedicate my life to yet, but it shan't be God and it shan't be some drip of a boy, either. I'm going to become a spinster just like you."

"A wise choice."

I could tell the Smurf thought I was saying one of those things I would change my mind about. It is true that I *did* change my mind about mayonnaise, but mayonnaise is not the same as having to wear some ghastly frock and stand perfectly straight for weeks on end in some sort of endurance test until someone asks you to marry them. I am simply not interested in being presented to the queen and then having to do a *season*. Marmalade said you have to go to a party every single night and dance until the soles of your shoes wear away for literally months. It's not that I don't like parties. I jolly well do. And dancing. It's more the finding-a-husband part of it. I mean, what if you don't *want* to find a husband? I asked Marmalade directly and she said it never occurred to her to question that part because she simply *exists* for grand romance. Which is all very well if you are the grand-romance type, but what if you're not?

We wandered through the park and to Mr. Lynam's art shop, where I bought some new pencils.

"The best person for Delphine, I think, would be someone who is away a lot so they don't have to talk to her very much. Maybe a major in the army or, you know, an explorer. Except explorers are usually quite exciting and Delphine has become *such* a martyr and a bore. She is *always* telling on me, for the most trivial of matters. I mean, surely you have noticed how all she does nowadays is sigh dramatically and moon about the place?"

Miss Smurfett dodged the question. "I think you miss Lady Delphine in the schoolroom."

I harrumphed and hopscotched past a woman who looked at me disapprovingly. "Shouldn't think so. We're better off without her, Smurf." Although a pang of missing the old Delphine did well up inside me, and I suddenly realized that if some porridge-faced boy really did go and marry her, I would be even more alone in the house.

At the Ritz we got honey sandwiches and crumpets and macarons, and I stashed some away for the interval. When we go to the theater, Miss Smurfett sits utterly still and takes in the poetry. And while she does that, I sketch. We sat in our usual seats. Mine has a hole in the back that looks like it was made by a knife. The Smurf and I think it is highly likely a spy killed a man by stabbing him in the back through the chair, during the war. Onstage, Lady Macbeth was wearing a plain black corseted dress. I carefully drew her face as she said, '*I heard the owl scream and the crickets cry*' and wondered what I would have dressed her in. Purple, maybe, because she wants to be a queen. I would have made her a crown out of the best costume jewelry, rubies and emeralds and semiprecious stones fashioned into thistles and eagles and Scottish wildcats. I would have woven tartan through it. I would have made her a cloak to wear through the castle at night and embroidered owls with amber eyes. I sketched these things next to her face to remind me. I like to lead a very disorganized life, except for my theater sketchbooks. I keep them in chronological order in an oak casket Father brought back from the Boer War. I alternate between red- and purple-bound leather and include the dates of all the performances I have sketched the costumes for.

By the time we got home it was really too late to even think of lessons. So we had a cup of tea in the drawing room, amid twenty gondolas Marmalade has had painted silver and gold with Italian poetry embossed in black all around the edges.

"Marmalade said I can keep a gondola for my room when it is over," I told the Smurf. I was just about to tell her I was going to have the gondola hung from the ceiling so I could sleep in it like a hammock when a noise like a sort of cross between a foghorn and the growl of an angry dog started to ripple through the house. Miss Smurfett put her teacup down and glanced off into the distance as if to pretend she couldn't hear it. Which was quite absurd because they probably heard it in actual Venice. As the third guttural wail commenced, the Smurf and I exchanged a look. It was the yowl of Delphine in anguish.

Miss Smurfett collected her carpet bag and politely left. I saw Mr. Corbet, the butler, and Mrs. Piercy, the housekeeper, discreetly disappear. But I am not one to run from drama. I climbed the stairs two at a time to Delphine's bedroom. The door was open. At first I didn't know where she was. All I could see was a huge pile of green fabric in different shades. It was as if the sheer amount of cloth had eaten her, like a giant sea monster, with her still alive and wailing within. Delphine and I are not often considered friends. She is a terrific do-gooder and obsessed with the most mundane of moon-brained things, so we mostly avoid each other. But sisters are sisters, and in this moment everyone else had politely vanished.

"Delphine." I tried to sound like one of the sisters in *Little Women*, a caring and homely type.

"Go away." Delphine was not fooled.

"I simply shan't."

She seemed to accept this and eventually appeared. She looked quite savage. Her face had gone completely purple and her tears were violent and not at all the attractive kind you read about in books.

"Everyone is going to laugh at me," she said, sobbing.

And when she looked at me, I stopped feeling my usual sisterly disdain for her, and a bit of my heart lurched. "Oh, Delph."

"I look . . ." She started to cry again and slowly, inch by inch, rose out of the sea monster until she was standing before me. For a second, even *I* was speechless, and that is jolly rare.

It was true. The ball she had been waiting for all her life was finally upon us. The ball that was supposed to be her moment in the sun. The ball that Marmalade had shipped in twenty gondolas and an Italian pastry chef for. And Delphine looked like a giant bowl of pea soup.

5

THE PENTHOUSE SUITE

Myrtle

Eventually, when there were so many trays of pastry stars and moons that they covered every single surface of the kitchen, Cook made us all a big pot of tea and some bread and butter. "Right, Dot, you take Myrtle to the attic and help her settle in."

"What attic?" Dot said. "Us girls don't live in the *attic*, do we?"

Cook rolled her eyes. "Not blooming this again."

"We *used* to live in the attic," Gladys said, cleaning flour off her glasses. "But now we live . . ." She stuck her nose in the air and flicked her hair and did a sort of royal wave. "In the Penthouse Suite."

Mary giggled. "Mr. Corbet's sister is a chamber maid up at Claridges Hotel. The top floor is called the Penthouse Suite. It costs a year of our wages to stay there for one night. And every single day they change the flowers. They had some Italian princess stay there, and they had to fill it every day at sunset with sixteen vases of fresh peonies."

"Sixteen," Gladys repeated, in awe.

Dot stood up and picked up my suitcase. "So nowadays our address is *The Penthouse Suite*—if you'll be getting letters sent here, you might want to let people know."

Cook started to busy herself with tidying. "Myrtle, I hope you are a bit more sensible than this lot. All day every day I have to listen to this giddy nonsense."

We wound our way up the servants' staircase, higher and higher. The last flight was so narrow I could barely fit my sewing machine up it. The corridor at the top sloped, with five little wooden doors off it. "That's the bathroom," Dot said, nodding her head toward the first door. "Mary and Gladys argue something chronic over who goes first in the morning. We only get one bucket of hot water between us, so the quicker you are, the better for the next person."

She walked to the end of the corridor. "We all wash our hair on Saturday nights. And then Cook makes us cocoa, and we dry our hair in the kitchen by the fire." She opened the door to the last room in the row, and I followed her in. It was small, but the late-afternoon sun bathed it in warm light. It shone through a little window, the frame painted blue, that looked out across the rooftops. There was an iron bed and a little chest of drawers, and on top of it, a vase with a peony.

The kindness of it hit me in a way I wasn't expecting. "Oh, Dot, how lovely of you, thank you."

"Welcome to the Penthouse." She smiled and touched my arm gently. "I'm so sorry about your pa. And that your ma is far away. But we'll look after you—we look out for each other here."

I sat down on the bed and snapped my suitcase open. "The last few weeks I kept telling myself I had to be brave. That I might be very lonely, but it would be worth it to make money to send back to Ma. I sort of felt like there could never be anything happy again." I looked out the window, past the peony and across London. "But maybe that's not true. This house feels like a happy one."

Dot opened a drawer and started folding my clothes neatly into it. "The duke and duchess are good people. At Christmas the duchess gave us all Liberty stockings, and she said Cook was to do us a spread that the king could sit down to. We had peaches and cream on Boxing Day too."

"The duchess is so beautiful," I said, and started to pin my favorite designs from *Vogue* and *Queen* magazine to the wall next to the bed. I took out my picture of Coco Chanel and hung it next to one of her most famous designs from last season.

"She could have married anyone, you know, the duchess," Dot said. "Cook told me the year she was a debutante she got one hundred and one proposals of marriage, and some from foreign princes and even the king of Spain. But she saw the duke at a ball in his military reds, and even though he was a widower with two little ones, she didn't care. Her parents were set on her becoming the queen of Spain and all that, but she told them that if they didn't let her marry the duke, she would lock herself away until she went mad. And then she went to her room and didn't come out for twenty-two days."

"Really?"

Dot shrugged. "Well, how would I know? But it's dead romantic, isn't it?"

I laughed. "Very."

Dot was looking at the pictures I had pinned to the wall. "You really do love fashion, don't you, Myrtle? The girl who lived here before, Trixie, she covered this wall in pictures of Rudolph Valentino, but look at you, with a whole wall of frocks. I still can't believe you made yours, it's a knockout."

She pointed at the picture of Coco Chanel. "Who's that, anyway?"

"She's a famous French designer. She came from nothing to build a whole fashion house."

"Well, Trixie didn't bag Valentino, but she did find true love with a bus driver called Sid and left here to marry him, so maybe you'll end up just like the French lady. Why not, eh? And anyway . . ." She pointed at Coco Chanel. "I think your dress is nicer than 'er one."

"I don't know, Dot. I'm good at copying designs and working out how things are put together, but I'm not so good at thinking of my own. I am hoping I can keep sewing, though, do some mending on the side to make a bit extra, maybe save up to bring my ma over for a visit. She'll be missing London—she always says she's a city girl, she loves the hustle and bustle."

Dot nodded. "Well, I'll be your first customer. I'd love a new skirt. You know, lady's maids need to sew, and they get paid more, so maybe you could work up to that? And later on, who knows? You're ever so talented. Right, I'll leave you to yourself for a bit."

She left, and I picked up my sewing machine and put it on the little table in front of the window that looked out across London. The first things I would make when I had a bit of extra money were some new curtains and a bedspread for the room—then it would feel a little more like mine. As I tidied things away, I thought about Ma being in Ireland when she really belongs in our shop in Stepney. I thought about the duchess knowing exactly where she belonged, with the duke. I didn't know where I belonged anymore, but maybe for now this house surrounded by cherry blossoms and filled with unusual people and laughter could hold me inside it for a little while. Things have to change for new things to happen.

I unpacked the rest of my clothes and put them away neatly. The last item I picked up was the parcel Ma had given me. It felt heavy in my hands. I unwrapped the brown paper and held the box for a moment before opening it: My father's best scissors. The ones his father gave him when they opened the shop. I held them in my hands and closed my eyes to feel all the memories that lived inside them. I put them on the bedside table so that every morning I would see them and remember who I am and what my dreams are. I looked at Coco Chanel and she looked back at me. For a second I imagined Ma back in our shop with our name over the door and a photograph of me in a newspaper wearing a dress I designed: "The new Coco Chanel."

I made my way back downstairs and into the kitchen. Cook was the only one there, and she was laying out a tray.

"Now then," she said, "are you feeling brave enough to take this up to Lady Sylvia?"

6

LOCH NESS DELPHINE

Sylvia

It felt socially unacceptable to be hungry. Delph hadn't mentioned food at all, and when the gong had sounded for dinner, it was as if she hadn't even heard it. And I didn't want to seem concerned with trivialities like self-preservation when she was very much in the throes of despair. It didn't seem very sisterly, either. But then at the same time, crumpets at the Ritz felt about five thousand years ago.

Together, we had wound her up in the dress like a huge ball of moving wool and pushed her through the gap in my bed-curtains. I have deliberately designed my bed so that it is impenetrable. My room is huge because it was originally built to be a cricket pitch until my great-great-grandfather found out it's impossible to grow quality lawn indoors. My bed is on a dramatic raised wooden platform you have to walk up steps to get to. My great-grandmother had it built, and every time you go to bed it feels like you're ascending the stage. On top is a giant four-poster bed. I took down the boring green tapestry curtains years ago, and now the bed is draped in my collection of fabrics: tartans from Scotland, jewel-colored silks from India, offcuts from ball gowns Marmalade has had made, and robes and wall hangings I found in the attic. It's so covered now that it's the perfect cocoon to harbor a distraught sister.

"You could run away. Don't you think that's even more likely to make you the talk of the town than the ball? I shouldn't think Marmalade would mind. She would love having a runaway stepdaughter. Or two . . . I do get dreadfully bored sometimes, so really, I don't mind coming."

I couldn't really see Delphine as it was entirely black inside the folds of the bed, but I heard her let out a tired little sob. Who knew Delph had so much to give in the boo-hooing department? I patted the bed until I found her arm and gave it a little squeeze. We both lay in the dark not saying anything for a while, but I listened as her breathing steadied and her shudders grew further and further apart. Just as I thought she was asleep, she spoke clearly into the dark.

"It's my own fault because I kept imagining it, but in my head when I imagined it, I was a different person."

"What do you mean? Who did you imagine?" She sounded resolutely mournful, as if her total humiliation had already occurred.

"Me, but a different sort of me. Shorter, not gangly and ridiculous. Confident, you know? Dazzling and beautiful, the type who makes witty observations and then, as she walks away, people say, 'Oh golly, isn't she just a scream?'"

"What sort of witty observations?"

"I don't know, Sylv, because I don't know how to make any." Her voice quivered. "Everyone always says Lavinia Andrews is—"

I sat up and harrumphed loudly. "Lavinia Andrews? You can't be serious, Delph. Lavinia Andrews is a clod. Remember that time I told her the boating lake in Hyde Park had a half monkey, half squid living in it and she believed me? What a—"

Delphine sighed. "Everyone says she is very beautiful."

"*Beautiful?* She looks like a half-witted mountain goat. Those huge vacant eyes and tombstone teeth. Delph, you can't think her a beauty. And she *can't* be considered captivating. All she talks about is the current temperature."

"At the ball at Pickford Place, everyone wanted to dance with her."

I tried to make her laugh. "Yes, just like people want to get a look at a strange museum exhibit, I should think."

Delphine chortled politely. "You're a good egg, Sylv. Extremely odd, but a good egg nonetheless." I heard her put her thumb in her mouth, which she only ever does when she's alone. "I was so embarrassed, Sylv. I could tell people only asked me to dance because they felt they had to. And only kind people spoke to me, like Albertine North and Victoria Lane." She started to weep very gently. "I just want to be one of the girls who everyone likes. Who giggles in the corner and hides from her chaperone, you know? Who can dance."

"Marmalade says dancing is all about confidence."

"That's because she is a wonderful dancer and the most beautiful woman in England."

Her sadness was so real I felt it creep up my throat and make my eyes sting. I crawled across the bed, lay next to her, and grabbed her hand. "What do you want to do?"

Delphine squeezed my hand in hers. "I just want to disappear. To not have to do it. The thought of it, having to make a grand entrance like Cinderella, and then dance with Fa in front of everyone and have my photograph taken . . ." She sniveled. "And everyone wants to be written about in *The Tatler*, and of course they won't write about me, because I am not beautiful or refined. And I *so* want to fall in love, Sylv, and that's what all this is *for*, but no one even wants to dance with me." More soft tears flowed. "But Marmalade has made such an effort. She wasn't keen on the stupid dress in Paris. But I insisted, and you know Marmalade, she said she would give me the moon if it made me happy. So now I'm going to have to go and let everyone laugh at me in this absurd dress. And watch them have a wonderful time at my ball while I stand alone at the edge."

I thought for a moment. "There are three days. Maybe you can have another dress made. Or we could alter it. Let me look at it properly—it might not be that bad."

I felt her nod in the dark, so I parted a piece of fabric, and we climbed out of the bed. She walked into the middle of the room and stood in front of the huge gold mirror. The dress was genuinely horrendous. It had giant rosettes all over it like the ones girls get at show jumping competitions, in the exact same shade of green as weeds that grow on the surface of ponds. At each shoulder was an even more giant rosette in shades varying from lime to overcooked cabbage. The bodice reminded me of a picture of Henry VIII I had seen in the National Portrait Gallery. All in all, it could not have been worse. Then there was a knock at the door. Delph flinched.

"Come in," I said. The door rattled slightly, and a girl I had never seen before walked in. She was petite with almost blue-black hair and dark flashing eyes. She looked about the same age as me. There was something steely about her. She was carrying a tray of sandwiches, and I had really never been so pleased to see anything in my entire life. "Hello. I'm Sylvia Cartwright, and this is my sister, Delphine."

Delphine tried to look ladylike and polite, but it was slightly ridiculous given she was dressed as a giant sea monster and as red and blotchy as a boiled lobster. "Are you new?"

She smiled very slightly. "Yes. I arrived today. Myrtle, miss." She curtsied—no mean feat while holding a full tray.

"Well, hullo, Myrtle. We are in the midst of an evening dress drama of classical proportions."

As Myrtle busied herself laying the tea things out on the table in the corner, I noticed she was wearing the smartest and most ingenious dress I had ever seen. She looked sharp, like she cut the air around her defiantly, like a film star playing a maid before she gets swept off her feet by a leading man.

It made Delphine's dress even more shocking. I couldn't imagine how it had all gone so wrong.

"They said the bustling would widen me. Make me less giraffe-like," Delphine said with a sniffle. The dress had flounces all over the waist and hips. They made her look like a maypole.

Every so often, I saw Myrtle look up from the grate, where she was making the fire, and glance at Delphine. I could see she was thinking intently.

Delphine and I discussed endless options. Get another dress made? There wasn't time. Modify one she already owned? Just brave the sea monster? Every time Delphine looked at herself in the mirror, the tears edged in again.

I took a bite of a cheese-and-pickle sandwich. "I wish I could help. I wish I could sew. I could draw you something wonderful, but I wouldn't know how to make it up."

At that, Myrtle looked me dead in the eyes, as if she desperately wanted to say something but didn't know how. Like she didn't know if she had permission to speak. But she turned around and kept sweeping.

She'd made me curious. "What do you think, Myrtle?"

She took a deep breath and stood up very tall, like she was being stretched. "Well, miss. I don't want to presume that I can help. But I do know a little bit about dressmaking."

7

A VAMPIRE COMES KNOCKING

Myrtle

My heart was thudding against my ribs as I made my way back downstairs. I could hear the chatter of the kitchen, but I knew I had to compose myself before I went in. As soon as I had told Lady Sylvia I could dressmake, her eyes had gone huge and she'd rushed over to me and whispered, "The fates must have sent you here to help poor, unfortunate Delphine. And she jolly well does need help, the lamb. She usually looks like that—like a giant daddy longlegs, I mean—but the dress seems to make her even more absurd, like a daddy longlegs in an Easter bonnet. Honestly, I know she must seem like a mortal fool, but Myrtle, she is my sister, and I simply can't allow her to be this . . . miserable." And then Lady Delphine had started crying again and Lady Sylvia had grabbed me and whispered, "Leave your light on. I'll come and get you later and we shall plot."

The idea that she would *actually* come felt impossible and unreal, but then something about the urgency and excitement that had surrounded her gave me a feeling she *would*.

I tried to clear my head and pushed the door open.

"So?" Mary gestured to the plate of biscuits on the table. "How was your first time upstairs? I couldn't believe it when I first saw the four-poster beds and the duchess's bath. I mean, I had to write my ma a whole five-page letter just about the bath. She still don't believe me that it's pink."

I took a biscuit and sat down. The kitchen was spotless. The production line of pastries, the flour-covered floor, and the huge simmering pots of caramel and custard and gooseberry fool had vanished. In their place were neat rows of shining copper pots and ordered utensils, ready to start the whole process again tomorrow.

"We were waiting for you," Gladys said. "We didn't want to go up without you. Not on your first night."

They were so kind. We chatted for a few minutes, then we tidied the biscuits away and trailed up to the Penthouse, where we each got changed in our bedrooms. Then we all washed our faces in the blue-and-white wash basin and stood in the corridor, brushing our hair out and braiding it for bed.

Dot's white-blonde locks hung to her waist unpinned, making her look like an elfin princess. She scowled as she brushed them. "Have you seen the list of things we've to do tomorrow? It's longer than the Bible. One of them is *make sugar gondolas for punch*. I ask you, what does that even *mean*?"

Gladys looked genuinely worried. "I was gonna set my hair, but there won't be time, not with all this. I mean, I'm gonna meet the queen, I don't want my hair outta place."

Dot snorted. "Gladys, you *might* get to offer the queen a glass of champagne, *if* they even let us upstairs. That is hardly the same thing as meeting her. And she ain't gonna be asking you for hairdressing tips, is she?"

"She might," I said. "She *has* had the same hairstyle for quite a while."

They all dissolved into giggles.

"Mrs. Piercy'll wake us at five," Dot said. "She's the housekeeper, and what she says goes. She is strict but fair. The rules are simple: look presentable, be as invisible as possible upstairs, don't speak unless one of the family speaks to you, and work your socks off. Sound about right, girls? Right, shall we let Myrtle have first wash tomorrow, to be welcoming? Then we do the morning jobs, but you're with me tomorrow, Myrtle—I'll show you what's what. Night, girls."

I closed the door of my little room. I felt like I had somehow lied to Dot and Mary and Gladys by not telling them about Lady Sylvia asking me to help her make a new ball gown for Lady Delphine. But what would they have said? I mean, it was laughable.

I looked out across the rooftops to the darkening part of the sky in the east. Leaving Stepney this morning already seemed like a fragmented memory, and that in itself was frightening. If home became hazy in my mind, then maybe Pa would too. Ma had given me the only photo she had of them both, so I opened the little leather case it was in and looked at them on their wedding day. Pa all handsome with dark curly hair and Ma in a long white dress she had made herself and a hat with roses around it. I curled up into bed and held Pa's scissors. What would he have said about today? About offering to help Lady Sylvia?

Slowly the whole floor became still and silent with the peace of sleep. My stomach bubbled. Sylvia coming felt wrong, like something I could get in dreadful trouble for. The very thought of her walking up to the attic seemed ludicrous. Did she even know where the maids' quarters were? What would happen if someone caught her? Or if someone caught me? I was listening so hard, I almost didn't dare to breathe, but in the end, I didn't hear her steps at all, just an ever-so-gentle tapping. Every part of me froze.

I slipped out of bed and crept to the door, still holding my scissors. I opened the door slowly, but as soon as I did, a hand grabbed me and yanked me into the darkness. As we flew back down the servants' stairs and out into a hallway of the main house I suddenly realized I was in my nightdress, but it was too late to do anything about it. Lady Sylvia, however, was wearing a long black velvet cloak with a huge swath of black lace over her head that reached right down her back like a train.

Sylvia pulled me up a narrow staircase into a part of the house that was so dark I could barely see where we were going. She flung open another door at the top of the stairs and launched us both through and into pitch-black. I heard the smack of a switch and then the room illuminated. We stood looking at each other. Me in my nightdress and her in her velvet cloak. She twirled. "Don't you just *adore* my disguise? What do you think I look like? A highwayman? Or a musketeer? Or—"

I surveyed the long cloak. "Well, yes. Or maybe . . . a vampire?" The lace veil covered her face entirely. "One who likes . . . beekeeping."

Lady Sylvia threw her head back and laughed. "A gothic beekeeper. Too, too funny."

We were in another attic room, full to the brim with an amazing assortment of things. Trunks were piled upon trunks, with labels like *Candelabras (16th century)*, *Bows and arrows (3rd Duke)*, and *Marmalade's doll hospital (gifted by Queen Victoria)*. There were old screens and dining chairs and card tables and a statue of a cherub eating from what looked like a pot of jam.

"No one ever comes up here," Sylvia said, "so we can talk in peace." She undid the fastening of her cloak and it fell to the floor with the veil, leaving her looking strangely unremarkable in striped pajamas. "Dashed heavy this opera cloak, I must say."

She pulled out some of the biscuits Mary had made earlier. "I stole these from the kitchen while in disguise. I can barely remember a day when I've eaten less. I'm mortally famished." And then she sat down on a chest labeled *Swords (various)*. Behind her there was a whole wall of suits of armor, just lined up, as if they were waiting for a bus.

For a moment we looked at each other, and then I quickly glanced back down.

"I'm sorry, Myrtle, to have dragged you into all this, but honestly, when you said you could dressmake, it felt like there might be an actual chance . . . to help Delphine. In the normal scheme of things, I'm not her biggest fan, but honestly, she is my sister and I can't bear for her to be laughed at, she simply doesn't deserve it. I know I am not some French designer, but I have been drawing costumes my whole life. I may not understand how clothes are made, but I understand Delphine, and I think I could draw something perfect for her." She became a little stiller, lost in her thoughts.

"It sounds odd, but when I am drawing clothes, I feel like a different person, like I am more alive than I usually am."

I felt something intangible travel through the air, connecting us. "That doesn't sound odd at all, Lady Sylvia. That is exactly how I feel when I am *making* clothes. I can see the different pieces of the pattern come to life in front of me. I *feel* how they should be cut."

Lady Sylvia looked almost relieved. "Do you think we can do it? Is it even possible? I know you must be awfully busy, with the ball and everything."

"I want to help, I desperately do. I miss making clothes, and my dream is to be a dressmaker. But I would get in dreadful trouble—I shouldn't even be talking to you like this. And, Lady Sylvia, even if I could help, there isn't time—the ball is in three days. Think how much work went into Lady Delphine's dress. There would have been a head of the atelier who interpreted the sketch and designed the pattern, and a toiliste who made a mock-up to work on, and then cutters and seamstresses . . ."

Lady Sylvia stood up. "Exactly, and look what a mess they made of it! How could they have allowed her to buy it? Even if we make her a potato sack, it would look better. I just want us to *try*. Myrtle, I think I can do my bit. I think I can draw something perfect, but do you think you can do yours? Do you think you can *make* it?"

My grip tightened around Pa's scissors. I knew the answer.

"Whatever you draw, Lady Sylvia, I can make."

She held out her hand to me. "So will you? Will you do this with me?"

I felt a tingle of fear and nerves shoot through me, but stronger than both those things was excitement.

I reached out and shook her hand. "Yes."

8

THE WHOLE WORLD IN A DRESS

Sylvia

The next night, I crept out of my room with the pile of news-papers I had stolen from Father's study, some scissors I had pilfered from Marmalade's dressing table, and *the dress*. I made my way to the east attic as silently as I could, and Myrtle arrived just after me, carrying her sewing machine. The day had seemed intolerably long; even the Smurf had commented that I was "*more* distracted than usual." But what Smurf didn't know was that I couldn't remember a time I had been more excited about something.

"I've been frantic with boredom, waiting," I said, and then felt foolish. Marmalade had said at dinner how hard all the staff were working. "Sorry, I mean, this ball must be the most outrageous chore for you all."

Myrtle arranged the newspapers I had flung onto the floor in a neat pile. "Everyone is excited about the king and queen being in attendance, Lady Sylvia."

A vague memory of having to go to the palace in an

itchy brown dress popped into my head. "*Really?* Well, they shouldn't be. Honestly, they are frightfully dull people. The queen only talks about children and how healthy or sickly they are. They made me go for tea there once and she said I had 'excellent teeth.' I mean, who talks like that, except the wolf in 'Little Red Riding Hood'?"

Myrtle put her sewing machine down and smiled. "How odd, thinking of the queen of England being like any mother on Stepney market."

We both peered down at the rather unpalatable mound of green fabric piled up on the floor.

"Oh, cripes, it is *dire*! I mean, every time I look at it, I think of the day Delphine vomited right onto her lap after reading a book called *Various Wounds and How to Dress Them*."

Myrtle squinted at the heap of algae-colored silk. "The fabric is exquisite, though. I think we can make something beautiful if we work all tonight and all tomorrow night. But first, we need to take it apart."

We stared at it intently, like we were examining a dead body or a particularly interesting fossil at the beach.

Myrtle crouched and started to sift through the various layers. "Let's try to hang it up. Although we really need a dressmaker's dummy."

Our eyes scanned the room and settled on the first duke of Avalon's suit of armor. "I shouldn't think he'll mind if we borrow it. He has been dead for seven hundred years."

We examined him together. "This one is a good height for a mannequin. He's the smallest and narrowest one." Myrtle was all sense. "But it looks very heavy."

"Do you think so?" I gave him a good shove and he unexpectedly lurched forward, an arm flailing out as if to grab Myrtle. I screamed and she jumped, and then his arm fell right off and his head jolly well did too!

The clatter rang around the room, and we both just stared at the headless armor, as if a man had actually been beheaded in front of us. "Gosh, you don't think he died in it, do you?" I asked.

Myrtle smiled. "No, I don't. If he'd have died in it, it would be buried on a battlefield somewhere."

"Oh, good thinking, Myrtle."

Still, we both looked inside the armor gingerly, just to make sure there was no skeleton inside. "It is awfully spooky, with no head, I mean."

We dragged the suit of armor upright, his other arm falling off in the process, and Myrtle held him up while I yanked him into the yards and yards of silk and chiffon. Myrtle took a step back to look at him and started giggling. And then I was helpless with hysteria too. The more we laughed, the more we couldn't stop laughing.

Eventually, Myrtle examined the dress again. "Lady Sylvia, the fabric is really beautiful. And there is *so much* of it. Enough to make four dresses if we needed to." She lifted up the top two layers of seaweedy silk. "And, look, the base garment is a wonderful color." She was right—the slip was a rich, dark turquoise.

"I know, I noticed it yesterday when Delphine was wearing it." A sudden unexpected shyness crawled up my throat. "I . . . I made a sketch of how it could look if . . . I mean, it might not be the thing at all."

"I would love to see." Her dark eyes were sparkling.

I handed her my sketchbook and my heart caught as she opened it. I felt in awe of Myrtle. I had met other girls my age at tea parties and ballet lessons, but I hadn't admired any of them the way I admired Myrtle. She radiated brilliance. She could actually *make* clothes, and she wanted to be something and had the guts to actually try and be it. I wanted her to like me and to think I could be something too. I didn't know what, really, but something different from what girls like me are expected to be. Myrtle turned the pages in complete silence and spent a long time looking at each sketch. When she finally turned to the last design, she looked briefly to the dress and then down again. I couldn't bear to watch her scrutinizing my work.

Myrtle looked at me, her dark eyes steadily meeting mine. "You are amazing. These are all breathtaking."

I felt something inside me trip. A sort of feeling of possibility, of change. "Thank you."

"It is perfect for Lady Delphine. The proportions, the simplicity. It's wonderful."

Myrtle whirred into action. "I can make this—*we* can make

Rosette
Headband

Lady
Delphine

Fancy
Fan

Cape train

this—but we will have to work incredibly hard. Tonight, we will have to dismantle the original dress so we have the fabric. I can draft a pattern for the new dress out of the newspaper, and we can fit Lady Delphine in the morning before breakfast. Then we can cut the fabric tomorrow night, and I can machine-stitch it together. You can help with hand-stitching the chiffon—mistakes will be less noticeable there, and I can show you how to do it. I think it is possible, but it will mean making the final alterations the morning of the ball." She looked up at me. "It will be close. And . . . Lady Sylvia, the dress is very valuable. Once we cut it there is no going back. I am new here, and I haven't been given permission to work on it."

"*I* am giving you permission. And besides, it's only a dress, even if to Delphine it is the whole world. It's not cutting a leg off. It's just fabric. Look here, I promise you, on my honor, you shan't ever get in trouble for helping me. If anything goes wrong, I will take the blame entirely."

She held the scissors next to the fabric, but she couldn't quite bring herself to make the first cut. I put my hand over hers and we did it together. A piece of green chiffon came away, and we both watched it as it snaked down to the floor.

"This is it," Myrtle whispered. "We're making the dress you designed."

Pride swelled inside me.

Myrtle showed me how to unpick the stitches and cut the cotton without touching the fabric of the dress. We worked in silence for the next hour or so, moving the armor gently and cutting away at the swaths of fabric. By the time the dress was stripped back to its slip, the floor was entirely covered in green, like a huge expanse of sea, and the first duke of Avalon stood headless and armless in a very elegant turquoise sack. My hands ached from the cutting and a lump had appeared on the edge of my finger.

Myrtle held her hand up. "I have a matching dressmaker's bump. Although mine never hurts anymore."

The bump felt like a badge of honor. I would soon be making something *real*.

I looked more closely at Myrtle's dress. The embroidery was so intricate and delicate. "Did you really make it?"

She nodded. "Yes. My father was a tailor. He taught me how to dressmake. Look . . ." She pointed at the scissors in my hands and then at her dress. "Those are his scissors."

"You really are heroically talented, Myrtle. Whose are the braids?"

"My best friend, Ethel. She taught me how to tango. She learned so she can be a film star. I wanted to know so I could work out how a dress for tango-dancing should move."

"You can tango? Crikey, Myrtle, you are so *sophisticated*. And I am jealous of you having a best friend. I don't really know anyone my own age. Marmalade doesn't approve of boarding school—she says girls always come out looking exactly like mashed potatoes. I've never even left the house without a chaperone, and you can make clothes that look like heaven and dance the tango."

Myrtle smiled and took a pencil out of her pocket. "Right, I am going to draw the pattern out on the newspaper, but I need you to help me with the details." She looked at my design and pointed to the bodice. "We will have to dart it so it fits her properly and moves with her." She put her pencil to my design. "May I?"

I nodded and she drew very lightly over my sketch. "Do you see? Here and here, there will have to be seams."

She handed me another pencil from her pocket, and I drew the bodice again, smaller next to the original drawing. "Like this?"

"Exactly." In bold, strong lines, she drew a large sort of rectangular shape on the newspaper. It looked like a child's drawing of a leaf. "That's the bodice panel," she said, and then drew a curved triangle. "And that's the neckline, do you see?"

She drew and drew, asking me questions about every detail of the dress, until there were dozens of pages of newspaper covered in strange shapes of different sizes. "It looks like an abstract painting," I said. "Or a puzzle."

"Yes, but when you fit it all together, it becomes like a sculpture, something curved and three-dimensional. It's a kind of magic, really."

It seemed impossible that all the unusual shapes could be sewn together to make something as detailed and real as the ball gown I had designed for Delphine, but the way Myrtle cut the fabric so confidently made me trust her.

We worked together until the sky was the very dark blue it turns just before the dawn. We looked out the window across the square. I couldn't see the moon, just the pink cherry blossoms dancing in the wind.

"How lucky you came here."

She gazed out into the night. "It didn't feel lucky yesterday morning, but you're right, Lady Sylvia, it does feel lucky now."

9

LADY DELPHINE'S DEBUTANTE BALL

Myrtle

Lady Sylvia was wearing an old-fashioned red military coat, with all the medals still hanging off it, and a pair of boy's cricket trousers. She should have looked ridiculous—in fact, had she been walking down the street, she would have looked almost mad. But as she marched up and down the room, she actually looked quite magnificent. Her hair was completely undressed; she had told me she had refused since birth to let anyone curl or put ribbons in it. It hung thick and straight to her shoulders and swung from side to side as she marched up and down the room. "Delph, come *on*. You do realize it is your debutante ball *tonight*. What are you *doing* in there?"

A strangled howl-yelp came from behind the bed-curtains. "I should jolly well think I do know." The noise curdled at the end and sounded dangerously like it might turn into tears. "I feel perfectly sick to my stomach."

"If you don't put the dress on, I shall come in there and murder you. I will murder you so completely that the only dances you shall be attending are the ones in purgatory. Because I'm quite sure they don't let people as lily-livered as you into heaven!"

There was a moment of complete silence when Lady Sylvia balled her fists together as if she might attack.

I took a step backward. "I'll go. If Lady Delphine—"

"You most certainly will *not* go. Not when we have worked every single spare minute to make this dress. Do you hear that, Delphine, you mooncalved fool? Myrtle has not slept a wink. She has dedicated every moment she has to making your dress."

I thought about the last three days. The endless jelly making and polishing and sewing golden stars onto great swaths of white fabric. And then the nights of taking apart the dress, drafting and cutting the pattern, and stitching and stitching to make Lady Sylvia's design come alive. We had started sewing it together last night at ten o'clock and finished at five a.m., just before Mrs. Piercy rang the morning gong. I had never felt so tired in my life, and we still had the ball to go.

"Delphine!" Lady Sylvia's shout was as deafening as it was enraged. "I am coming in right now and I am going to—"

But just then a chink in the bed-curtain appeared and one ankle after it. Lady Sylvia and I exchanged a look. And then Lady Delphine took one step and then another down the stairs until she was standing in the middle of the room. She looked completely different. Even barefoot and with her hair undone, she looked quite breathtaking; the dress had transformed her. Only someone of her height could have pulled off the simplicity of the neckline and cut. It hung completely straight, but the silhouette of the line made her look elegant and exciting. It was unapologetically brave and glamorous, and somehow only she could have worn it. When you dressmake you have to give people the thing they most need when they wear the outfit. Lady Delphine needed to feel beautiful, and the dress certainly made her look it.

Lady Sylvia was speechless. And then, quite unexpectedly, she threw her arms around her sister. "Delph." She led her to the mirror. "Look, Delphine, look at yourself."

Lady Delphine took a breath and then raised her head and stared at herself. Her hands trembled ever so slightly as she turned one way and then the other, letting the draping splay out behind her. A tear rolled down her cheek. She spoke to my reflection behind her. "Myrtle, it is so beautiful. I look so . . ."

"Beautiful," I said. "You look beautiful, Lady Delphine."

She shook her head. "But I'm not really, I mean, *I'm* not a beauty. Your dress just makes me look—"

"Don't be exasperating!" Lady Sylvia cut across her. "Look at yourself, Delphine. That *is* you. That is how you look."

"I'm just . . . terrified. It is so daring. Everyone will look at me and . . . I just don't know if I can do it. Honestly, I can't imagine actually wearing it, not tonight. I just don't know if I am the type of girl who can wear a dress like this. But, Sylv, it is so clever of you to have drawn it, and Myrtle . . . I am in awe." She looked at me. "Thank you, sincerely. From the bottom of my heart."

I curtsied ever so slightly. "I truly loved making it, Lady Delphine."

Lady Sylvia snorted. "Would you stop harping on about not being able to wear it? If you don't stop, I will simply never talk to you again. And I will personally ensure they carve 'ball dress coward' directly onto your gravestone. 'Here lies Lady Delphine Cartwright, who could *possibly* have been interesting but chose to be a bore.'"

"You are so full of death," Lady Delphine sniveled.

"If only I could say you were so full of life," Lady Sylvia flashed back. "And besides, you have nothing else to wear, so unless you are planning to go naked or run away this instant, you jolly well better find some courage."

I dismissed myself to return to the kitchen and ran to put my apron back on. I jumped down the stairs two at a time. We had done it, and it felt different from anything I had made before. Lady Delphine's dress wasn't about practicality like the dresses back home. It wasn't made to last until it fell apart; it was made to capture a perfect moment in time. I understood Lady Sylvia's designs; they were different, stories with character and emotion that I had to make come to life. And I had done it. *We* had done it, and it was perfect.

Belowstairs was an explosion of people and cooking and hysteria. It was all-out bedlam. "Did you have a good break?" Gladys looked deranged. She was covered in flour from head to toe—even her glasses were thick with it—and on her head was a tied handkerchief, covering up the dozens of curls being held tight with pins underneath. "That's the last one." She held up a small quiche triumphantly. "That's the five hundredth salmon and pea parcel. Myrtle . . ." She put her hand across her mouth and whispered, "When Mrs. Piercy dismisses us to make ourselves presentable, come to Dot's room."

I nodded and glanced over to Dot and Mary, whose heads were also covered in handkerchiefs, and got back to polishing the sherry glasses. My hands had gone bright red with the sheer amount of scrubbing, polishing, and sewing they had done over the last three days. My dressmaker's bump had gotten even bigger.

The next hour passed in a blur, and then Mrs. Piercy made a rousing battle speech about not looking any of the guests in the eye, being seen and not heard, and "making England proud."

We almost fell over each other running up the stairs, and in the end we all had to wash at once, as there was only enough time to boil one bowl of water. We stood in our slips, washing behind our ears and getting giddy as fish. "Even if the princess Mary is just near me, I will faint on the spot." Gladys was impassioned. "Do you think we will *feel* her in the room? Her royal being?"

Dot and Mary started to madly curtsy to each other, the very low royal curtsies we had been practicing all week.

"You're up, Myrtle." Dot grabbed my hands and led me into

her room. "Come on, girls, we can't have Myrtle miss out on looking like a film star for the queen of England."

Before I knew it, three pairs of hands had shoved me into a chair and were madly grabbing sections of my hair. I couldn't see the setting lotion, but the smell of it was so overpowering, my eyes stung. Within fifteen minutes I had a scarf on my head too, and we were away polishing our shoes and pressing our dresses with the huge iron Cook had heated on the stove for us.

My stomach was bubbling with anticipation an hour later when the gong went. I wanted to do everyone proud; they had been so kind and welcoming. And I couldn't wait to see the ballroom all lit up, and the couples dancing, and, most of all, the dresses. We lined up for Mrs. Piercy to inspect us in the hall. She walked along the line of staff, adjusting a lapel here and a cuff there. Her footsteps stopped as she turned to the four of us, and her eyes rested one by one on our identically waved hair. She opened her mouth to speak, but the sound of the first carriage pulling up stopped her. The night had begun.

10

THE MOMENT ONE'S LIFE BEGINS

Sylvia

No one noticed me clambering up into the attic, because literally every single human being in the house had been sucked into the ball goings-on downstairs—even people who had no interest in being sucked into it, such as the coachman, whom Marmalade had persuaded to dress in Venetian livery and stand in the square holding a lantern, and Father, who was wearing a quite absurd purple silk evening jacket entirely against his wishes. Marmalade had persuaded the whole household, and dozens of people she had hired especially to help, into a rainbow-colored whirlpool of a Venetian extravaganza. And I was not going to miss it. I had been told a dozen times I was too young to attend. Marmalade had even arranged for me to have an entirely chocolate-based feast in my bedroom to soften the blow. But if they thought I was going to sit in my room with the greatest ball of the century going on downstairs, then they were barking.

I have one of the best collections of theatrical costumes

outside of the Lyceum Theatre, and it was time to put it to good use. Once my uncle Cecil was playing Prince Henry at cards, and he bet him any costumes from the palace collection he wanted. The next day I was the owner of a whole lion, a fireman's suit and hat, a beanstalk, and twelve dancing princesses' gowns.

Finally, after rummaging in five different boxes, I found what I was looking for. I sneaked back to my bedroom and tied the Venetian mask, stolen from the schoolroom, around my head. The brightly colored stripes of the clown costume and the huge red buttons on the front matched exactly with the swaths of material Marmalade had hung from the ceiling of the ballroom. I looked like a circus performer, bare feet and all. I did spare a thought for what Father might do if he found out. Girls are not allowed to attend balls until they have been presented to the queen, so really it would be very shocking if I were seen, and Father would have to punish me severely by sending me to boarding school in Switzerland or something. But then, in truth, I'm not really one for pondering the future, so I bowled straight ahead.

I sneaked down the servants' stairs and into the ballroom. It looked breathtaking. The gondolas, silver and gold, were dotted around the edges of the room and filled with huge silk cushions. Silver and gold stars hung down amid the colorful silks, and there were bright silver birch trees and tables and tables of food. At one end of the room a stage had been erected, and the biggest band you've ever seen, all dressed in rainbow silks, was playing a polka. Every chair on the edge of the dance floor was filled with chaperones: people's mothers, aunts, and bored fathers. They were pointing at each and every one of Marmalade's inventions—the tower of champagne glasses, the Italian love poetry painted in gold all over the walls, the citrus grove—and the boundless energy of the debs and their delights. I could see the queen in navy satin and wondered what she was thinking. If Marmalade's aim had been to make her sick with jealousy, then I should have thought it was game, set, and match to her. I spotted Father, did a cartwheel across the dance floor away from him to keep in character, and saw Myrtle holding a tray of pineapple tarts in the corner.

It is hard not to notice Myrtle. It's not even to do with the way she looks. It's a sort of poise she just naturally has that makes you feel like she is a cut above. I took a biscuit and she smiled politely.

"It's me," I hissed.

"I know," she hissed back.

"Why didn't you say hello?"

"Because I am working." She kept her eyes fixed ahead of her. "And in any case, you are in disguise."

"Not a very good disguise if you recognize me."

"Yes, but I *knew* you were going to come in disguise, so it doesn't quite make me Sherlock Holmes, does it?"

I shrugged and took another four tarts. "Have you *seen* her?"

Myrtle discreetly shook her head. "I have been watching out for the last hour or so. You do think she's coming, don't you?"

"To her very own coming-out ball? I should think so. I mean, if she doesn't show up now, on my honor, she will be the first deb ever to enter her ball dragged in by her own hair!"

And then everyone went silent and looked up to the entrance. Marmalade's ornate arch of Venetian oleanders, lilies, and violets, gently illuminated by gold candles in Venetian glass orbs, framed the top of the staircase wondrously. Quite inexplicably my stomach started to knot, and my cheeks went bright red underneath my mask. Suddenly, rather than wanting to murder her, all I wanted was for Delphine to survive her grand entrance.

"The duke and duchess of Avalon," Corbet announced, and the room politely applauded.

Marmalade looked as beautiful as ever, but noticeably understated, in a dress the same purple as Fa's jacket and her smallest tiara.

"Lady Delphine Cartwright." Myrtle and I exchanged a look in spite of ourselves.

And then she was there. Standing in front of three hundred people, dazzling, daring, and utterly transfixing. The simplicity and elegance of the dress was fresh. It made every other dress in the room seem gaudy and babyish. The acres of girls in pastel flounces and frills seemed ridiculous now that Delphine was standing before us. The richness of the turquoise silk hinted at a sophistication and confidence that only I knew Delphine did not possess.

Even Marmalade's beauty was momentarily dimmed by the resplendent shock of the entrance. Fa took Marmalade and Delphine by the arm and led them into the ballroom, and then a man approached my sister and bowed. Marmalade looked quite wild with triumph.

"I say, who is that man, the one asking Delphine to dance?" I demanded of a nearby woman holding a chow chow dog, who seemed taken aback that a circus performer was asking her a question.

"Why, the prince George. How could you not recognize him? So handsome . . ."

"Well, all males look broadly the same to me."

I could tell from the way Delphine was breathing and the tension in her mouth that she was nervous, but nobody else would have noticed.

Delphine and the boy reached the center of the room. "I feel awfully queasy," I said.

Myrtle smiled and shook her head. "Don't. She is going to be wonderful. I can feel it."

As the waltz began, neither of them said anything. Each time Delphine spun, the pale green wisps of chiffon we had sewn to the shoulders of the dress flared out behind her. And as she slowed in time to the music, the sash around her hips and its long train snaked around her like smoke. She wasn't a show-off and she never would be, but she looked like a film star. But more than that, underneath the tension of the dance and everyone admiring her, I could tell she was happy. Because she was there, at her ball, dancing with a "deb's delight," just as one was supposed to.

Out of nowhere, Marmalade waved at the chow chow lady and started to cross the ballroom. I picked up a tray of glacé pineapples arranged in a dome and tried to look like I had been employed by her to hold it. Myrtle was cool as a cucumber.

"Oh, darling Mrs. Fenton." Marmalade was shaking with glee. "I am simply wild with elation. Delphine is a triumph."

"Indeed, she is, Lady Cartwright. Her dress is so very modern. Is this what the ladies are wearing in Paris? I know you went there to choose it."

"Yes, we did indeed go there to choose it," Marmalade said, and then she picked up a tart from Myrtle's plate, looked at her directly, and very slightly raised an eyebrow. "But dear Mrs. Fenton, as you know, I have always said that, while in Paris they do know a thing or two about dresses, you simply cannot beat a London tailor." She took a bite of biscuit and spoke very slowly. "Delicious, Myrtle, you really are a girl of *many* accomplishments."

Myrtle curtsied but maintained her composure. "Thank you, ma'am."

Just before Marmalade shimmered away, her eyes flickered over me for a second longer than one might expect, and then she was gone.

The room dazzled with color and glamour and music. I saw

a girl in flounces take Delphine by the arm and lead her into a gaggle of girls. And that pot of poison Lavinia Andrews was cooing over her and Albertine North was hugging her like her dearest friend, and it all seemed worth it. It wasn't socially acceptable for a duke's daughter to dressmake, and scullery maids certainly didn't rustle up debutante ball gowns. This would have to be our secret. But I knew it would burn inside me always. And *we* knew we had made the dress. All by ourselves. A ball gown that had wowed an entire room.

Something was fizzing inside of me, an excitement I hadn't ever felt before. I saw Myrtle's eyes follow Delphine out of the room. "Marmalade told me once that she knew the exact moment that her life began, that she felt it in a ballroom on Berkeley Square. Do you think this is our moment? That our lives are really beginning?"

Myrtle looked as if she were thinking thoughts a million miles away from the lemon grove and champagne-filled ballroom. "I feel like nothing has happened as I expected it to recently, and this is just another unexpected thing. A good one, though. The first good thing. Thank you, Lady Sylvia. I really loved making Lady Delphine's dress."

I looked at her. "Honestly, Myrtle, this has been simply the best week of my life."

She smiled at me, a huge joyful smile. "Me too," she said. And the band struck up a tango.

11

FOOTLOOSE AND FANCY-FREE

Myrtle

"As I live and breathe, girls, would you cop a look at this!" Dot shouted as I walked into the kitchen. She was at the table polishing champagne glasses, because even though it had been a week since the ball, we were still getting the house straight again.

Mary and Gladys rushed in from the cold larder and even Cook came through from the pantry.

"You've finished your outfit." Gladys beamed. "And in time for your day off. You're a knockout. I wish I looked like you, Myrtle, and could bleedin' sew like you too."

Every evening after supper, the girls had played cards and I had sat with them, chatting along, making a new outfit for myself. Ma had given me the fabric for my birthday last year, and I had finally decided what to make with it: a proper grown-up lady's day suit.

"Where you going, then?" Dot said. "All dressed to kill."

"Just back to Stepney. I want to get some fabric to do my curtains and maybe enough for a bedspread too."

Geometric Embroidery

Purple Ribbon

Dot reached into her apron and started counting out her pennies on the kitchen table. "And don't forget my skirt fabric. Nothing fancy, just som'ing that makes me look like a film star so all the fellas fall at my feet."

Cook clipped Dot with her tea towel. "Poor Myrtle. What else do you want from Stepney, Dot, a winning lottery ticket and an around-the-world trip? Have a lovely time, love, but mind how you go. Going home can be sad as well as 'appy."

I waved goodbye to them and went to Mrs. Piercy's office.

She looked up from her desk. "You look very presentable, I must say, Myrtle. A credit to us, you are."

Then she opened a huge heavy book and in neat spidery handwriting underneath Dot's name wrote *Myrtle Mathers* and in the next column *scullery maid.* I signed my name, and she gave me a little brown envelope with my wages in it.

"Now, don't go spending it all at once. Half for you, half for mother, is it?"

"Yes, Mrs. Piercy."

"She must be very proud of you."

I nodded, thinking to myself just how proud of me Ma would be if she could see what I had made this week. And especially if she knew that a dress of mine covered a whole page of *The Tatler* magazine.

I felt the pocket of my coat to check if it was there, and then almost ran through the cherry blossoms and across the square to the park. I found a bench, took the magazine out of my pocket, and looked at it for the thousandth time.

Lord and Lady Cartwright hosted Lady Delphine's debutante ball at home at Serendipity House on Saturday last. The ball was a triumph and certainly one of the most spectacular and decadent *The Tatler* has ever attended. Lady Delphine looked simply divine in an ingenious and quite beautiful gown that has set the tone for the whole season to come.

And there was Lady Delphine. In black-and-white she looked older, more poised, and quite beautiful. They had chosen a full-length picture to show the dress more clearly. Lady Sylvia had told me it was the only full-length photo of a gown featured in the whole society section.

She had tapped on my door just past midnight and hurried across the house and up to another part of the attic, where we had read the article aloud to each other endlessly and stared at it in disbelief. We both agreed it was the very greatest thing that had ever happened to either of us. Lady Sylvia had said it was to be the first chapter of her story, because this certainly wasn't going to be the *most* exciting moment of her life. There were going to be many, many perfectly thrilling chapters to come. To me it felt like the colors of my dreams were becoming brighter and clearer. Like suddenly I had a map that was beginning to fill with roads and possible directions. I *would* save enough to bring Ma back for a holiday, I felt sure of that now. Lady Delphine had already given me a whole ten-pound note, and I was making extra doing bits and pieces for the girls. And if I could make a dress good enough for *The Tatler*, then one day, surely, I could be a professional dressmaker too? When I was making the fires or darning socks, I would daydream I bought our shop back for Ma. I would imagine her behind the counter again, serving customers, smiling from ear to ear. And then my dreams would wander to even bigger things: Sylvia and me making clothes featured in magazines with our names written underneath, just like Coco Chanel.

I went to the post office and posted my letter to Ma. One day I would tell her about the dress, but not now when it was so new, because she would only worry I would get into trouble — after all, we had cut up a startlingly expensive French couture evening gown without permission from the people who paid for it. And I couldn't tell her I had become friends with Lady Sylvia. Even though our paths rarely crossed in the house now, and even though we might never speak again, for those few days we had been friends. The dress had connected us and made us feel like equals. But in the world outside clothes, we weren't equals at all. I wasn't even supposed to speak to Lady Sylvia unless I was spoken to by her, and if anyone knew otherwise, I would be in deep trouble indeed — maybe even sacked.

It was a windy day, but I sat on the top deck of the bus back to Stepney anyway. I didn't have to walk this time, because I had money in my pocket I had earned myself. London looked so happy against the bright blue sky, and all the way home, I daydreamed about dresses I could make and the fabrics I might buy. Eventually, the view changed to buildings I knew and shops I recognized and a kind of longing came back to me. A longing for home.

I hadn't really meant to walk back to the shop. I had thought I would get the fabric at the market and avoid seeing the shop at all, but when I got to Stepney, I couldn't help it—my feet just followed the familiar cobbles and turned the corner. The shop had been painted a glossy black and in smart gold lettering was *Trent and Son Tailors*. I watched an old customer of ours walking out holding a pair of trousers, and it stung a little. Then a boy a couple of years older than me, wearing a tailor's apron, walked out the door. I stared at him in disbelief. Because in his arms, like a baby, was Schiaparelli! *My* cat. The cat we had given to Mrs. Crimps, our neighbor, to look after. I watched from across the street as Schiaparelli jumped onto her favorite cobble and rolled over to have her tummy tickled. Schiaparelli the *traitor*, allowing herself to be stolen by the people who had bought the shop from under us, and *enjoying* it too. I indignantly marched across the street without a clear plan of what to do when I got there.

The boy looked up at me from his tummy-tickling position and then stood. He was tall and had brown hair flecked with blond, and blue eyes. He waited for me to say something, but when I didn't, he just said, "Erm . . . can I help you?"

I didn't know what to say, so I folded my arms and scowled—and then Schiaparelli finally realized who her true owner was and launched herself into my arms. She nuzzled into my neck and I melted.

"Steady on, Tweedie," the boy said.

"*Tweedie?*" I almost spat.

"She loves to sleep on the tweed, you see."

"I know she does. I made her a tweed kitten blanket. Her name is Schiaparelli, and she's *my* cat."

"Oh." The boy was quiet then, and I started to feel a little silly for having gotten cross. But the boy didn't seem to have noticed at all. He broke into an enormous grin as if something truly wonderful had happened. "You must be Myrtle. Everyone who comes into the shop talks about you." He looked at my suit. "And we still have that fabric at the back. I should have realized. Come in, come in. I'll get you a cup of tea. And what was it again . . . *Schiaparelli*? Tweedie can have some milk."

I didn't know if I could face going into the shop; there were too many memories. He seemed to sense my hesitation. "I'm Stan, by the way. And honestly, I could do with your help. I'm in a bit of a pickle."

I followed him in, and the smell was so familiar it took my breath away. To some extent, the shop was the same as it had been when I left it. The wooden counter filled with different colored cotton reels, the back room with its sewing machines and towering piles of fabric rolls. But it had become an utter mess. The rolls had all been pulled out, and fabric was cascading down the walls in huge waves. The cutting table was strewn with tools, and the counter was covered in cups and saucers and old receipt books. I looked disapprovingly at

Schiaparelli, who had overseen this descent into chaos. She skulked away to the pile of tweed in the back corner.

A woman laden with shopping bags came in and said, "Just a yard of canvas, please."

Stan looked in one cabinet and then another and then inexplicably climbed the ladder that led to the shot silks and started rummaging around hopelessly.

"I mean," she shouted to him after a long moment, "do you just expect me to wait here until I meet my maker?"

"Navy or white?" I asked.

She looked me up and down. "White."

I walked behind the counter, took the white canvas out of its drawer, laid it out, and cut her some without measuring.

"A penny, please," I said, and the woman handed it to me.

She looked Stan up and down. "Men!" the woman said to me, and shook her head as she left.

I handed him the penny and he looked a bit sheepish. "Oh, Myrtle." He swung himself up onto the counter. "As you can see, I ain't really the tailoring type."

"Where's your father?"

"He's left me in charge," he said, rolling his eyes. "He's gone up to Scotland to buy tweed for next winter. He says I've got to learn how to run things if I'm gonna fill his shoes someday."

I surveyed the shop.

"And as you can see, it ain't really going that well. I don't even want to be a tailor, you see." And then he stood on the counter and jumped off it, straight into a Charlie Chaplin roll.

"*I* want to be an actor, but my dad reckons that is stupid. Anyway, I hear you're quite the actress yourself—Mr. Boots from the fruit stall came in here to get a shirt made and he said you used to do cracking impressions. Made me feel quite inferior."

I went a little red. "Not really, I . . . It's just something me and my dad used to do to pass the time when the shop was quiet."

"Go on, do one."

I put my hands on my hips and then started clapping. "Roll up, a dozen apples, today, only tuppence."

"That's Mr. Boots, all right! You sound exactly like him. Do another one."

So I did. We stayed all afternoon in the shop, doing impressions of all the different people we knew from the market and famous people as well.

Stan was so funny, in his movements and his jokes, and he was a good mimic too.

We drank tea and I served customers and tried to teach him a thing or two about the shop.

"It's a right shame that you have to be a maid and I have to be a tailor, because we could make a great music hall act," Stan said.

I laughed. "I don't want to be an actress; I want to be a dressmaker. I am still making things for people on the side, you know. But I want to do it for a living one day, properly." I could feel the magazine cutting in my pocket.

"Well, I tell you what," he said. "When I'm a famous Hollywood star, I will buy all my suits from your fashion house." He fell into another Charlie Chaplin roll. "I reckon movers and shakers like us need to help each other out."

"Sounds like a fair deal to me."

I bought the fabric for my curtains off him and some pink cotton for Dot's skirt, and we said goodbye. "Thank you," I said. "For looking after Schiaparelli Tweedie."

"Anytime, and remember, I'm here if you need anything. It must be hard, not having the shop anymore. I'm sorry you had to sell it."

"That's kind of you to say. And as for the shop, you'll get the hang of it—eventually."

On the bus back to Serendipity House I thought about Pa in the shop, showing me how to run it, and it was the first time I had thought of him without having to push away tears. Being back in the shop with Stan had been fun. Maybe going home had been more happy than sad in the end.

It was past teatime when I walked back across the square. Just as I turned to enter the servants' entrance, Lady Sylvia jumped out of a bush in front of me.

"Myrtle," she hissed. "Thank *goodness* you're back. Agapantha Portland-Prince is *here*. To see us! Both of us!"

12

COUSIN CALYPSO FROM THE COUNTRY

Sylvia

"What do you mean?"

Myrtle looked almost affronted. She was *maddeningly* un-up-to-date. Which wasn't her fault, really, given she hadn't been present for any of it. I grabbed her hand and yanked her behind the large orange rhododendron that a suitor had hauled all the way from China for Marmalade in a quite stupid act of love.

I lowered my voice to a daring sort of whisper. "Agapantha Portland-Prince is sitting upstairs in my room right now, drinking tea and eating bourbon biscuits, and is simply *mad* to talk to us about designing her some clothes."

Myrtle's eyes widened slightly.

"I don't know who that is," she said. "And what do you mean . . . *both* of us?"

"Well, obviously both of us. *We* were the ones who made Delphine's dress. Only *we* can make ol' Agapantha's."

Myrtle looked worried. "But how does she know? That we

made Delphine's? I thought Delphine promised not to tell anyone."

"Oh, don't worry about that, Myrtle. Agapantha is a comrade. I haven't seen her for years, but the last time I did was at a country house party. Anyway, I wanted to see if I could fit my whole body into this ancient vase in the library, which I bally well *could* as it happens, but then I stood up too quickly, and the whole thing toppled over and smashed into a trillion pieces. Then, when the maids and all that ran in, Agapantha said it was a gust of wind from the east that just toppled the thing over. And then we both got hot chocolate and treacle sponge for the shock. Agapantha can keep a secret, all right."

"Lady Sylvia, I could have gotten in severe trouble last time. I am a maid. I shouldn't even be having this conversation with you. I shouldn't have helped with Lady Delphine's dress; I didn't have permission."

"Nor did I. I really don't see where waiting around to be given permission to do things gets one. I'm not going to ask someone's permission to feel alive."

"I'm new here, and I'm only just finding my feet. Mrs. Piercy is very clear about what is and isn't allowed. I love making clothes, but I can't enter into something like this, not with you."

She carried on walking, but I caught her arm. "Myrtle, please, wait a moment. Listen, ever since we made Delphine's dress, I have been drawing like mad. I used to sketch costumes, but now I draw other types of clothes too—ball gowns and day skirts and coats. It used to feel like a silly hobby, but now it feels different, like something special. I want to feel that feeling again, the one I felt when Delphine came out in our dress. But I can't do it alone. I have never met anyone as talented as you, Myrtle. You made what I drew magical—don't you want to do it again, together?"

"I would love to make a ball gown with you, but I can't risk my place here."

"I won't let anything bad happen to you, I promise . . . and Agapantha is riddled with money, so she will pay you well. No one would know it was you—how could they? I mean, it's the most unlikely thing on earth, us two designing dresses together."

"Agapantha will know—"

I tried to be casual about the next bit, as if it were neither here nor there. "That's the thing, she won't. I just knew you would be worried about telling Panth you are a maid, so I told her you're my cousin Calypso from the country and that you would be back from tea at the Ritz at any moment. Don't you see, I have created the perfect cover for you."

Myrtle looked genuinely shocked. "Lady Sylvia, that's deception, I can't! If anyone found out—"

"Please stop calling me Lady Sylvia. You are my friend. Actually, my only real true friend, so you must call me Sylvia. And no one will find out. We don't have time to discuss it. Meet you in my room in five minutes." I squeezed her hand and launched myself out from behind the rhododendron and back around to the front of the house.

The main thing we needed to do was seem grown-up. Agapantha had to trust us and believe that, even if we were young, we could do it. So I opened the door dramatically and swept in, like a heroine taking the stage.

Agapantha looked like a girl in an advertisement for swimming costumes, all tall and bronzed and strong. She put her teacup down. "Thanks awfully for seeing me, Sylvia."

I affected the mannerisms of the hostesses I had seen in action. "Agapantha, *darling*, please don't get up." I slightly danced across the room, allowing the sleeves of my great-grandfather's fencing shirt to billow, and sat down. "Cousin Calypso is just freshening up—she won't be a moment."

I wasn't entirely sure if she would arrive at all, but then on cue there was a knock and Myrtle appeared. She had tied a lilac scarf around her head and let it drop right down to her waist, like a French artist. If she were a deb, she would be the main competition for every girl without even trying.

"May I present my cousin, Lady Calypso Mortimer?"

What Myrtle was feeling on the inside was imperceptible. She glided across the room with casual certainty and shook Agapantha's hand. "How do you do?" she said.

She sounded completely different; her whole speaking voice had changed. I couldn't quite believe it—her cockney accent had vanished. She sounded just like me!

"Gosh, I do *love* your outfit," Agapantha gushed.

79

Myrtle smiled graciously. "It's one of my own designs."

Agapantha wouldn't have noticed that she didn't say, "I made it myself," but I did. Myrtle always chose her words carefully. I thought I might have to nudge her to sit down, as a guest would, but she played the part to perfection. I handed her a cup of tea, and she sipped it genteelly, her ankles crossed neatly, her elbows perfectly tucked in. I have never, ever cared to be graceful, and always preferred to be daring rather than chic, but Myrtle made me wonder if I ought to think again. She was truly much better at being a lady than I was.

I reached over and squeezed Agapantha's hand in a chummy fashion, as I have seen Marmalade do so many times when she wants to know the gossip. "So! Tell us *all* about Delphine being a triumph."

Agapantha's face lit up. "Gosh, it is quite the talk of the cocktail parties and mothers' luncheons. I promise you, everyone is aquiver with it. You know how people love an unexpected plot twist—well, Delphine is quite the corker of one. People are saying Bertie Foster himself asked to be the first on her dance card at the Dorchester last night, and he is the most eligible bachelor in the whole of England, according to my mama."

An unexpected and previously dormant sense of pride in Delphine welled up inside me. I was about to say she had become quite obnoxious with it all—she was forever mooning about now, applying Pond's Cold Cream and lying around on chaise longues, wistful. But I stopped myself; perhaps Agapantha was longing to moon about the place too, lusting after Bertie Foster, whoever he was. But then Agapantha was a very different kettle of fish from Delphine altogether. She wasn't shy. She didn't have the painful awkwardness and horror of being the center of attention that Delphine did. She didn't seem like she needed a dress to make an impact.

Then a most curious noise came from the carpetbag she had put down next to her chair. She saw the look of confusion on our faces and laughed heartily. "Don't worry, that's just Queenie."

The strange sound came again, a cross between a meow and a pigeon's coo. She reached inside the bag and pulled out a very small brown creature with a furry mouselike face, part koala and part hamster.

"It's a quokka. My brother Caspian brought her back from his travels in Australia. She got caught in a hunting trap when she was a baby quok, poor thing, and she was too injured to go back into the wild, so he kept her. Do you know they are one of the only creatures on earth, besides us, that can properly smile?" She proceeded to tickle the creature under its chin, and it did indeed break into the widest, jolliest grin. "I usually leave her at home, but I've been out so much with all this deb carrying-on, I think she's getting bored. She rather chewed the drawing room curtains last week in an act of rebellion and Father wasn't at all happy. Especially considering he is already spending *heaps* on my ball."

"Is that what you need your outfit for, your ball?" I asked, offering her another biscuit.

"Well, not exactly. Mama seems set on this quite frightful woman doing it. We went to her studio, and she actually looked away when she saw me, as if her eyes were affronted just by my height and air of clumsiness. And then she said I needed to practice walking and that I have unfortunate hands. I mean, bit of a rotten thing, to say I can't even *walk* properly." The quokka jumped onto the tea tray, picked up a custard cream, and started chomping it down. "The thing is . . ." She glanced from side to side as if to check the coast was clear. "I have the most outrageous secret and I need your help keeping it."

13

ESCAPE FROM MOUNT OLYMPUS

Myrtle

"A secret! Really?" Sylvia jumped up in excitement. "Are you eloping?" She clapped her hands. "Do you want us to make your wedding dress?"

"No, nothing like that. I don't want to marry anyone, ever. It's a much better secret than some boring old romantic drivel."

Sylvia screwed up her face as if she were thinking very hard and then shook her head. "Nope, can't think of anything. Unless you are a spy or something, on the side?"

Agapantha looked at Sylvia and then back at me. "Sylv, I know you are the greatest of shakes in the secrets department. Delphine told me you made her dress and never told a soul about it. And I haven't forgotten that time when we were small and you kept quiet about Pickles having kittens. You know I still have all seven? Father just thinks it's one cat that looks different depending on the lighting." She looked at me with her warm, open face.

"But what about you, Lady Calypso? Are you good at keeping secrets?"

Sylvia's eyes went huge, the hint of a giggle forming at the sides of her mouth. She turned around and shoveled a sandwich in to stop herself. "Oh, I can vouch for Calypso when it comes to secrets, all right," she garbled through her sandwich.

I straightened my skirt over my knees and made sure I looked poised. If Agapantha was good at having secrets, then she was probably good at keeping other people's too. If she ever found out I wasn't Lady Calypso Mortimer, I could hope she wouldn't tell anyone. But that didn't make what I was doing less risky. If Mrs. Piercy ever found out I had actually pretended to be someone else, and an aristocratic lady at that, I would be dismissed without a reference or pay. It was an unimaginable level of deception and audacity. But it was my chance to keep making clothes, and maybe even buy the shop back for Ma one day.

I took a sip of my tea as if there were really nothing on my mind, and then I thought about the way posh people spoke— clipped and taut and without moving their mouths very much. "I promise you, Agapantha, that I am a most excellent secret keeper."

"Well then, hurrah!" Agapantha reached down and rummaged around in her bag, pulling out a copy of *Explorer* magazine. She flicked to a well-thumbed page. "Look." She held it up and pointed to a double-spread advertisement.

I read it out loud.

> Volunteer explorers wanted for a zoological expedition to the Amazon to categorize native wildlife. No fieldwork experience necessary. Sound knowledge of the animals of South America and orienteering expertise essential. Men between the ages of sixteen and fifty welcome to apply. We sail on the *Star of the North* from London on June 28th.

Sylvia looked slightly confused, but Agapantha was triumphant. "Well, guess who has been accepted on to the expedition and is running away to South America?"

"What?" Sylvia scanned the magazine again. "But, Panth, how can you have been accepted, you're not a—"

"Oh yes I am and oh yes I have! I applied pretending to be a seventeen-year-old boy named Periwinkle Smith, and they have accepted me! I got the letter yesterday just before I saw Delphine. She told me all about her dress, and now here I am. That's right, I am jolly well running away!"

Agapantha's bombshell bounced around the room. Sylvia was standing perfectly still, just staring at Agapantha, mouth agape, half a sandwich still in her hand.

"Running away," Sylvia repeated. "Panth, how . . . simply *marvelous* of you. Are you *really* going to? I mean, I should think your parents will go perfectly loop-the-loop."

"Well, it's their fault. I mean, they just won't *listen*."
Agapantha stamped her foot. "You see, I'm *mad* for animals,
always have been. At home I have dogs and cats and the
horses, of course, and Queenie. But it's more than that. I have
read all the zoological books at the British Museum Library.
I can identify all the different species of the different conti-
nents. I know their Latin and their English names."

"Gosh! Brainy!" Sylvia exclaimed. "My governess, Miss
Smurfett, would adore you. You know women are allowed at
university now, don't you, Panth? They changed it."

"I know, and I begged my parents, but Father won't allow
it. I told them I want to be a zoologist, but they just refuse to
listen. All Mummy does is plan my ball and read about who I
might marry in *The Tatler*."

I looked at Agapantha in her practical but perfectly made
blue wool day suit. If I had seen her walking down Oxford
Street, I would have thought she had everything you could
ever want. And didn't most girls long to be exactly what
Agapantha was? A deb, being presented to the queen and
doing her season? Endless balls and society photographs and
a handsome deb's delight at the end? She would never have to
work a day in her whole life. Gladys would probably sell her
soul to the devil just to do Agapantha's season for her.

"The thing I am wondering," I said politely, "is how can
Sylvia and I help you?"

"Well, there are things I *need*, and I can't very well ask
our tailor to make them. I mean, I would pay you, of course.

I need a tweed suit for traveling and a safari suit for when I get there, and shirts, pajamas, and ties. The thing is, Mama watches me like a hawk, but she won't suspect a thing if I'm popping over here all the time. I mean, Delphine is the toast of the season, after all. So . . . what do you think?"

Lady Sylvia looked a little crushed. Men's suiting was probably not what she had had in mind. But I thought about the hours I had spent with Pa on trouser pleats and shirt buttonholes and suit linings, him by my side, showing me again and again all the different techniques. I was lucky I had had a dad who wanted me to be able to *do* things. "No problem at all—we can make you all of those pieces."

"Can you really? How perfectly marvelous!"

Queenie jumped into Agapantha's lap and up onto her shoulder. "Well, at least my ball is two days before my escape. Mummy goes pink when she talks about it, she is so excited. Honestly, I think she cares about the ball far more than she cares about me. I should have felt very bad if I'd had to exit stage left before it even happened."

"What is the theme of your ball, anyway?" Sylvia asked, leaning down to tickle Queenie under her chin.

Agapantha groaned. "Horrors! This theme business is simply too, too mortifying. You know Maud Rilance's one tomorrow is called 'A Pastoral Scene.' Mother is making me go as a sort of shepherdess, with an actual *crook*, as if the whole thing weren't too sick-making already."

"The more I hear about being a deb, the more I think

I am going to jolly well wriggle out of it," Sylvia said.

"Too right! And do you know what my theme is?" She snorted heartily. "Mount Olympus. And of course, Mummy wants me to go as Aphrodite. I mean, can you imagine anything more deathly? She might as well put a sign on my head saying, 'Marry her, please!'"

"But, Panth, Mount Olympus is *brilliant!*" Sylvia cried. "I mean, just *think* of how jaw-dropping your costume could be."

Sylvia was quite clearly thinking about it herself, and with pure excitement. I could feel her whole energy change because her mind was alive with it. She marched up the stairs of her bed and stood at the top. She was still in her long riding boots, jodhpurs, and scarlet jacket, so she looked quite imposing. "Look here, Panth, we will make you all your boy clothes, the whole lot. And we will be true comrades to the cause of helping you run away. But on one condition: we get to make your debutante gown."

Agapantha shrugged. "Fine by me. I don't care about the dashed ball anyway. But if you can have a condition, then so can I: I want to wear trousers."

14

THE SPIRIT OF FRIENDSHIP

Sylvia

At eleven a.m. precisely, Delphine, Marmalade, and Father all filed into my room with Morton, the gardener, and Lawson, who runs the stables. I had persuaded Morton and Lawson to engage in the technical aspects of actually hanging the gondola, so it seemed like the right thing to do to invite them to its party. Miss Smurfett was also present but did not look entirely comfortable in the yellow oilskin fisherman's coat and rain hat I had found her. Both Marmalade and Delphine wore suits and hats for the occasion. I was wearing an admiral's uniform, complete with medals, and a general's hat that I had found in the attic. Father said that since he had never been in the navy, his army sash would just have to do. The gondola hung on ropes from either side, about six feet from the ceiling, with a rope ladder hanging down to the carpet. I had wound floral garlands up each rope and filled the gondola with bright silk cushions. In huge, slightly uneven writing, in the same red as the ladder, I had painted its name.

I grabbed the bottle of champagne and climbed the ladder, stopping at the top.

"That had better be my cheapest bottle!" Father barked.

"Father, take your hat off," I said, "out of respect."

Father did so, and Lawson and Morton followed suit. I stood at the top of the ladder with the bottle in my hand.

"I hereby name this gondola *The Spirit of Adventure*."

"Bravo!" Delphine whooped.

I held the bottle up.

"Remember, not too hard, darling!" shouted Marmalade as I smashed it against the side of the boat. Fizz exploded everywhere as Father and Delphine dodged pieces of falling glass.

As soon as the final shards of glass had been swept away and my bedroom door was shut, I set to work. I wanted to make the gondola a brilliant surprise for Myrtle. It was the perfect place for us to keep our things where no one would find them: a swinging hideout in midair. A place where I could sketch and where we could meet in the night and work on our designs together. A piece of the world that belonged to just us.

I climbed back up the ladder, rung by rung, the weight of all my costume diaries in their wooden box almost making me topple backward. I had been sketching as much as I possibly could, but nothing seemed quite fabulous or glamorous or witty enough. It would be the first time ever that a deb had worn trousers to her ball. It would be in all the magazines—Agapantha was the duke of Wellington's niece, after all. I was desperate for it to be so startlingly magnificent that no one ever forgot it. I had begun to feel that it could reset the whole course of my future, *if* I could get it right. I climbed back down and fetched my charcoals and paints and carried them up again, and then finally the very last thing—a huge, brand-new leather-bound sketchbook with a little padlock and key. I nestled up against the silk cushions, letting the gondola rock gently back and forth, and took out a pot of gold paint and a paintbrush and started doodling letter shapes on a piece of scrap paper.

As soon as I heard Myrtle's quiet knock on the door I lay down.

"Come in!" I shouted.

I heard Myrtle turn the handle and walk in. I could feel a giggle welling up inside me as I imagined her peering around the room below for me. It exploded as I popped up.

"Boo!" I shouted.

"Sylvia, it's amazing! I couldn't imagine it before, but it's like a magical flying canoe!"

"Come up! I have another surprise for you."

Myrtle climbed the ladder with her usual grace and stepped onto the gondola. She sat completely upright, surveying the room, then turned and looked out across the huge window, over Green Park, to the city.

"London doesn't seem so big when you are up here. I can almost see Stepney."

I realized for the first time that I had never thought about what it must be like for Myrtle to be so far away from everything she knew. The shame of it made me blush. We both looked out the window for a moment in silence.

"Terribly selfish and un-comrade-like of me never to have asked you if you miss home. You must, awfully." The words stumbled out awkwardly.

She looked distant for a second, her dark eyes unfathomable, staring across the treetops of London.

"I miss a home that isn't there anymore. I miss a memory." She shrugged.

She was so regal. In her black dress with her black hair framing her dark eyes, she looked like Cleopatra sailing down the Nile.

"I bought us something," I said. "I spent all my birthday money on it at Mr. Lynam's. I had been saving it for costume sales, but now that life has taken a turn for the frantically exciting and we are making costumes, I don't really need to buy any."

I turned and picked up the huge leather sketchbook. "It's a designer's book. It has special overlay pages for the pattern cutter's notes. I thought we could put Agapantha's outfits in it. Do it properly."

Myrtle took the huge book, laid it on her lap, and turned the key in the lock. She ran her hands over the thick cream card on the inside and smiled.

"It's lovely, Sylvia. I've read about these. Parisian designers have them. The key is to lock the collection book so nobody can steal your designs."

"Ours has two keys, one for each of us. It's yours just as much as mine. Without you, it's just pictures. I can draw *anything*—stardust, mermaids' tails, dinosaurs, a vampire cow, a dazzlingly wicked witch—but *you* can make it actually appear."

"Well, I can't do vampire cows, but a dazzlingly wicked witch maybe."

"*A dazzlingly wicked witch*," I said dramatically. "It sounds like a novel."

"Or a film with Gloria Swanson," Myrtle said, giggling.

"Yes! Gloria dressed head to toe in black with white stars." I sat up and took a piece of paper and started sketching. Myrtle watched as I drew. "And maybe a long opera cloak in velvet with a mink trim that fans out behind her as she breaks Gary Cooper's heart into a million pieces."

"Yes!"

I quickly drew a velvet cloak with a dramatic upturned collar. Myrtle tilted her head and looked at the page.

"Maybe a star-shaped clasp at the neck, made entirely of diamonds."

"Diamonds that Gary Cooper brought back from his travels to win her heart," I said, and swooned back onto the cushions.

I handed her my piece of paper, and she took a pencil and drew arrows to each thing I had drawn. Quilted panne velvet. Wire-weighted collar and hem. Felted stars, trimmed in silk. I watched her draw an arrow to the dress and write *taffeta* and then a question mark.

I stood up, and the gondola rocked toward the window. I plunked myself down next to Myrtle and reached for my pot of gold paint and paintbrush. She moved the designer's book from her lap so it was half on mine too. We both looked down at the blank leather cover. I dipped the brush into the paint and tapped off the excess. I looked at Myrtle.

"Shall we put our first names or our surnames?" I asked.

"Our surnames," Myrtle said decisively. "That's what shops have."

I let my paintbrush swirl across the cover in big, flowery script: *Mathers and Cartwright.*

"It does sound a little like a solicitors'," I said. "I think it's because we're not called something glamorous. 'Coco Chanel' has a bit more of a ring to it, really."

Myrtle picked up the brush and painted cherry blossoms falling gently down the cover, and then wrote across the middle in gold *The House of Serendipity.*

15

AN UNEXPECTED VISITOR

Myrtle

"Shhhh, or she'll hear." Mary shut the door of the cold larder, and it went pitch-black, which just made us giggle more.

"How am I supposed to light the blinking thing if I can't see it?" Dot squealed, but then there was the sound of a match striking, and we were all faintly illuminated in the darkness. Dot started lighting the candles.

"Have you got the present?" Mary whispered.

"Yes." I had wrapped it in an old piece of blue cotton and tied it neatly with string.

"What will *I* do? If Dot has the cake and you have the present?" Mary said.

"Oh, my giddy aunt." Dot handed her the plate with the lemon pound cake she had baked that morning. "You carry the cake, I'll just be the amusement."

Dot opened the door of the cold larder, got a wooden spoon and a pan off the dresser, and started banging them together. "Roll up, roll up, it's only Gladys Staples's birthday once a year, you know!"

We walked down the hall and into the kitchen, where Mrs. Piercy, Cook, and Mr. Corbet had stopped what they were doing, and even the groom, Mr. Peters, had stepped in from outside. Gladys, who had been kneading bread at the table, went bright pink. "Oh, you didn't have to."

Dot led a riotous "Happy Birthday to You," pan bashing the whole way through. Mary put the cake in front of Gladys, and she blew out the candles in one go.

"Now, don't go telling that gossip what you wished for," Cook said, nodding toward Dot.

I put the present down in front of Gladys. "It's from all of us."

Gladys carefully unwrapped the blue parcel. "Oh, my goodness." Her eyes went wide as she picked up the dusky pink silk blouse. "It's so beautiful. I've never had anything so perfect."

Dot gave her a hug. "Mary and I got the silk. Mrs. Piercy let us off to go up to the market and get it. Everyone put a bit toward it. But Myrtle made it."

Mary ran to the kitchen show dresser and opened a drawer. "Look." She opened *Picture Show* magazine. "It's just like Greta Garbo's, exactly the same."

Everyone peered over it, even Mr. Corbet. Greta Garbo stared enigmatically into the distance, all dark lips, arched eyebrows, and waved hair. Her blouse was long, with tucked pleats on the right side and three pieces of the same silk that hung from the neckline to the bottom of the hem. The end of each was covered in small crystal beads that were replicated on the cuffs.

"I helped with the embroidery," Mary said. "Myrtle showed me. I did the right cuff on my own."

Gladys beamed. "Thank you all." She looked at me. "Honestly, Myrtle. It's a dream. I can't believe it."

Cook handed out plates and put the kettle on the stove, and we all sat down round the big table.

"And now Myrtle's made the pattern, we can all 'ave one," Dot said.

"The poor girl!" Cook said. "Give her a break. She'll be dead on 'er feet just so you lot can swan around pretending you're Greta Garbo."

"I don't mind, honestly." I didn't. Making Gladys's blouse had helped me practice pattern-cutting and tucked pleats again, but the happiness it brought her alone made the hours I had spent on it worth it.

We heard the familiar clip-clop of horse hooves on the cobbles outside. "Finally, the milkman's here," Cook said, but when she opened the door, it wasn't the milkman at all.

"Stan!" I couldn't believe it. "What are you doing here?"

"Well, I thought I'd come and see you." He smiled in his easy way and tipped his hat to the whole kitchen full of people. "Pleased to meet you all, I'm sure."

"Is this your friend from home, Myrtle?" Mrs. Piercy said kindly. "Well, why you don't you invite him in for some birthday cake?"

"Cake, yes, please. Born under a lucky star, I was," he said as Cook handed him a slice. "And happy birthday." He grinned at Gladys, and she went pinker than her new blouse. Dot and Mary were nudging each other under the table and suppressing giggles. Mrs. Piercy gave them a sharp look. "Well, Stan, it's lovely to meet you."

"I wish I could talk with you properly," I said. "But I've got work to do."

"Nothing that can't be done in half an hour's time," Mrs. Piercy said. "Not when this young man has come all the way across London to see you. So, just this once, why don't you go for a little walk, show Stan where you're living."

"Well, it don't look too bad so far," Stan said. "I mean, it ain't got the charm of a two-up two-down in Stepney, but you know, I could live 'ere at a push."

I took off my apron and hung it up.

Cook handed Stan some carrots. "For your horse. Myrtle'll show you where the water is if it needs a drink."

We wandered out and to the stables, where Stan had tied up a dappled gray pony. I fed her the carrots as Stan got her a bucket of water. "She's called Spots," Stan said.

He picked up a huge box and set it down at my feet. "I brought you a present."

"It's Gladys's birthday, not mine." I felt a bit embarrassed by his kindness, that he had come all this way, just for me. I opened the box. "Oh, Stan."

It was filled with dressmaker's patterns. Blouses, dresses, skirts, even swimming costumes and petticoats. I recognized them all—they were Ma's that she had left in the shop because she couldn't take them away with her.

We sat down on a hay bale. "We only do men's tailoring," Stan said. "We don't need any of these. And anyway, they were in the shop when we bought it. They're yours."

There were other things in the box too: collar molds, bodkins, needles, seam unpickers, cotton reels in dozens of colors, pinking shears, and chalk and thimbles.

"Anything we had a duplicate of, I put in," Stan said.

All I could think looking through it was how much time it would save me making Agapantha's outfits. "Thank you, Stan. Honestly, this is just the loveliest thing. Maybe I was born under a lucky star too." For a short moment I thought about hugging him, but then shyness took over.

"You're gonna do it, Myrtle. I know you are. One day all the fancy ladies are going to be wearing clothes you've made. It seems all wrong, me working in your tailor's shop when you're the one who wants to be a tailor."

"Don't suppose you fancy swapping? I think you'd look good in a footman's uniform."

He laughed. "Nah, waiting on toffs isn't for me."

"Thank you, Stan. I'll be so much quicker now. I've already got commissions." I opened my mouth to tell him about Agapantha but stopped myself. The fewer people who knew, the better, and I didn't want Stan getting wound up in something as potentially scandalous as the duke of Wellington's niece running away.

"I might send you a list of fabrics. I need some gaberdine

and tweed and canvas. I'll pay you for it."

"Course, anything you like." He stood up and straightened his back and held his arms up. "I'm learning to ballroom dance. I reckon it'll help me become an actor, you know, at auditions and things." He did a few steps. "Care to join me?"

I shook my head and felt my ears burning with embarrassment. "I'd better get back to work."

It felt good to have had a visitor from home, a new friend from an old place.

Later on when I went back upstairs, the leather book was waiting for me under my pillow. Sylvia had finished the design. I shut the door and sat on my bed with the tiny key in my hand. This was it: our next design. Our chance to make something spectacular. As I turned the key in the lock, I felt a swirling inside me. I thought about Coco Chanel and Madeleine Vionnet and wondered if they had felt it too.

My heart surged as I turned the page and then I saw it. If there had been any part of me that doubted Sylvia's sheer genius, it disappeared. It wasn't that it was daring, beautiful, and magical, even though it was all those things. It was that it was completely different. A kind of evening wear that simply didn't exist. But as well as that, it captured who Agapantha was and what she wanted to be: brave and free.

I locked the book back up and went back to the kitchen, the energy still swirling inside me.

16

PERIWINKLE SMITH'S BIRTHDAY

Sylvia

"Do you know, before I met you, I don't think I've ever been awake at sunrise. How strange, when I must have been awake for sunset every day for my whole life."

I clambered onto the chest at the end of the attic, and Myrtle climbed up beside me. Through the tiny window, we watched the sky go from pale bluish-mauve to warm apricot. I leaned my head on Myrtle's shoulder, the tiredness of being awake all night gently creeping up on me.

Myrtle yawned an elegant, dainty yawn. "All we need to do now is the seams on the tweed trousers and the lapel stitching on the safari jacket. The lapels really ought to be finished by hand, in the pick stitch I taught you."

She went and sat down at her sewing machine. I watched her fold the trousers three times to make sure the seam was correct. Her whole being radiated a preciseness that fascinated me. Even her hands seemed to have more poise and control than the average person's. They moved quickly but never seemed to make a mistake. I watched her wind the bobbin up and start to run the fabric under the needle. I went and picked up the trousers and clambered back onto the chest. The attic room had become a workshop. Every single one of the suits of armor was dressed in some item of clothing or another. The third duke was now wearing a set of striped cotton pajamas and the seventh a lightweight summer shirt and lilac silk tie.

The whole of the attic floor was covered in offcuts of fabric, newspaper that Myrtle had made patterns with, thousands of pieces of cotton, and what looked like half a dozen porcupines crawling across the floor that were actually pin cushions. Myrtle had made two suits from scratch. Watching her do it had been mesmerizing. And I had helped. She had taught me how to cut out the pieces of the pattern with a steady hand against the floor and how to hand-stitch seams and details. Agapantha's traveling wardrobe was almost ready.

We folded the clothes into a neat pile.

"Try and get a couple hours of sleep before Panth arrives."

Myrtle nodded sleepily. "At least it's my day off today."

"And what a day it's going to be! Do you think Panth will pull it off?"

"I really hope so. If she pulls it off today, I reckon she's in with a shot of making it all the way to the Amazon."

I crept back to my room feeling positively exhausted but elated by everything we had done too. I took a running leap and hurled myself through the air and onto my bed, where I sank into the cushions and soon fell asleep.

I awoke to Agapantha climbing the ladder to the gondola in a very nonchalant fashion, one-handed, while eating a macaron.

"I say, where did you get that?" I mumbled through a sleepy stretch.

"Look, there's a tray over there."

And so there was—good old Mrs. Piercy never lets me down when I miss breakfast. There was a whole tray of sandwiches, biscuits, a jug of juice, and some fruit loaf. I scooped it all up into the tablecloth, swung it over my shoulder, and climbed up the ladder myself.

"Mother's gone barmy," Panth said, shoveling in a cucumber sandwich. "She's having grapevines hung from the ceiling in the ballroom."

"I think that sounds jolly fun. Better than that one Delphine was telling me about where some goats wandered in and ate the curtains and the bottoms of everyone's dresses."

"Oh no, I thought that one was too, too *darling*. Lady Astor let me keep a goat, you know, Sylv. I named her Bridget Betsy Parkins. Mother was desperately cross when Betsy got into the car home with us, but now she lives in the most divine little yellow house we had built just for her."

Myrtle knocked and came in holding the design book. It

was her day off, and she was wearing an outfit I hadn't seen before: red art silk made into a drop-waist dress, trimmed in white, with a white silk bow stitched flat at the collar. She was wearing a white wool beret in the exact same shade as the bow and was carrying her coat. She really did look like an absolute knockout.

"Gosh, Calypso, you look absolutely *darling!*" Agapantha lurched over the side of the gondola at the same time as me, and for a second I thought we both might fall out. She plonked herself next to me to make room for Myrtle, tipping the gondola like a seesaw.

Myrtle ascended the ladder with her usual grace.

"Right, now we are all here," I said, reaching for our design book. "Are you ready to see it?"

"Too right I am. I went to my other fitting with Mummy, and the dress the woman is making me, *honestly* . . . you know the way meringue has that choppy edge to it? Well, the whole dress is like that. A huge choppy sea of pink meringue with my head sticking out of the top of it. I don't know how Mummy can think it *attractive.*" Panth giggled. "Poor thing will get a frightful shock when I appear in my *actual* costume."

A jolt of nerves shot through me. It had taken me so long to think of it and get it onto paper. I wanted it to be everything that Agapantha was: brave, unique, and utterly *herself.* I wanted it to show the world what Agapantha Portland-Prince was really made of. And I wanted her to love it too, and recognize herself in it, the way that I did.

Poseidon Costume

Agapantha

Queenie

I opened the book and laid it on her lap.

Agapantha traced her fingers around the edge of the sketch and then read each of Myrtle's notes individually. The gondola rocked violently as she fiercely hugged both of us. "You've done it! I love it. It's *perfection*. I honestly cannot wait to wear it!"

We trooped back down the ladder and then we handed Agapantha her tweed suit. Myrtle and I both watched as Agapantha Portland-Prince disappeared through the bed-curtains, and someone else entirely stepped back out.

A tall boy in a tweed suit, blue tie, and bowler hat emerged, beaming from ear to ear. The disguise was so flawless, neither Myrtle nor I could quite speak. "Well, you had better wish me happy birthday," Agapantha said. "Because today Periwinkle Smith has truly been born."

17

DRESSED FOR FREEDOM

Myrtle

I stood very still behind the servants' curtain to the drawing room, where I could just peep in on what was happening. Our plan was for us all to go shopping together, to get the things we needed for Agapantha's costume, and to see if she really could pull off pretending to be a boy. But none of it would happen unless Sylvia could convince Marmalade to let her miss the luncheon party being thrown to celebrate Delphine's season.

The drawing room was probably the most beautiful room in the house. Serendipity House seemed as if it belonged in the pages of a fairy tale. The duchess's dress mirror was covered in roses that wound around it and made her look even more like a fairy queen. The paintings were all of far-flung lands, full of flowers and animals I had never seen before. Every vase I picked up to dust felt enchanted; every time I touched an ornament, I half expected a genie to appear. Dot, Mary, and Gladys just saw it as endless things they had to clean, endless things they could break and get into trouble over. But I loved it. They made me feel as if I belonged somewhere magical and new.

Only yesterday Sylvia had put two medieval chairs on either end of the ballroom windows and used the damask curtains to swing back and forth between them. She moved about the house chaotically, arms and legs flung out at random as she danced through all the spaces she inhabited as if they were alive and would know to move out of the way as she spilled into them. She didn't fear them like Dot, Mary, and Gladys; she positively owned them, without ever really seeing how wonderful they were.

Now she swept into the drawing room and flung herself down onto the silk cushions Dot spent hours pressing every week. They were in a war that Sylvia had no idea existed. Dot would plump the cushions through gritted teeth, and Sylvia would always walk in on cue and destroy them again.

The duchess was wearing a long yellow knitted jumper and matching skirt and was practicing her golf swing. "Darling!" She looked up. "What a frantically witty outfit! You are too clever."

Sylvia had decided the best way to successfully go out in London without a chaperone and without rousing suspicion was to pose as a French woman. She said as soon as people thought she was foreign, they would not even think to remark she bore a resemblance to the duke of Avalon. I was going to manage the fabric buying, and Agapantha was going to do all the talking in the shops that stocked the items she needed for the expedition. We had planned it meticulously, but now that I was standing listening to Sylvia execute the plan, my stomach started to churn. Pretending to be Lady Calypso Mortimer outside of Serendipity House felt like a much bigger risk. What if one of us saw someone we knew?

For her chosen role of *French woman definitely not Lady Sylvia Cartwright*, she had pulled out all the stops. She had spent hours turning a Moroccan rug into an elaborate full-length coat, with matching hat and bag. The effect was somewhere between a genie and an enormous bouquet of flowers. It was the first time she would ever have been out without a chaperone, and she was on fire with it.

The duchess swung the golf club and almost hit a huge vase of flowers. "Honestly, little Sylv, do you see any point in this new fashion for exercising? Seems awfully silly to me, to dig tiny little holes in the ground so you can try and whack balls in them, but Lady Astor told me it's all the rage, and you know how I like to be on the cutting edge of things. Is darling Agapantha still here? I so want to ask her for all the deb gossip; Delphine is like a sphinx, she tells me *nothing*."

What Sylvia and I both knew was that Agapantha was waiting in the garage in her brand-new suit. Sylvia didn't miss a beat.

"Oh, Marmalade, she *can't* come in. She's absolutely"— Sylvia looked at the ornate yellow ceiling for a very brief moment before pursing her lips and sighing dramatically— "phobic of mustard."

"Gosh! How whimsical of her. I personally think it's delicious. Is it because it's French? Do you know, before the war, I fell in love with the most dashing Frenchman for three whole days. He gave me an entire beetroot for lunch, quite on its own, and then took me to the *naughtiest* part of Paris to dance." Lady Cartwright threw her golf club down and giggled. "But I'm not smuggling any mustard, I assure you, Agapantha, darling," she shouted in the general direction of the entrance hall. "Do come in."

"It's not the *food* mustard," Sylvia said. "Well, it *is* that. But it's also all mustard things. Including the color." She then slowly looked round the room, to the ornate mustard silk wallpaper and deep mustard curtains and affected a frown. "Too, too unfortunate."

"Indeed." Lady Cartwright smiled to herself. "You know, when I was a girl, I took a solemn vow not to say the word *cheese* for a whole year. Just to see if it was possible."

"Was it?"

"Oh yes. It was very character-building, now I think of it, what with all the cheddar in the world and whatnot."

Sylvia had roamed extremely far from the task at hand, and suddenly seemed to realize this.

"Anyhow, Marmalade, listen here. I know you said we have to have luncheon with this trifle-faced fool who's got the hots for Delphine."

Lady Cartwright's eyes twinkled and she picked up her

teacup and stirred her tea slowly. "Bertie Foster. I do, indeed, remember inviting him to luncheon. He would be such a wonderful match for your sister."

"Well, I want to be excused. You know how I hate long meals where I have to say things about the weather and sit up straight for eternities. Remember that time with the Hepworths and the troll . . . incident."

Whatever the troll incident was, the duchess clearly did remember it, as her eyes narrowed slightly. "I hope you would not ruin your dear sister's chances of matrimony with theatrical impressions of flesh-eating mythical creatures."

"Well, I shouldn't mean to, I never do . . . but . . . the risk could be avoided altogether . . . if I were, geographically speaking, somewhere . . . else. Like the theater?"

"The theater, you say? With the Smurf? Well, as you know, I do not believe in education through boredom, especially with maps and fractions and things, but you must become accomplished, and the theater is educational indeed. I'm sure your father would understand the need for you not to neglect your studies."

Sylvia ran over and gave her a kiss. "Thanks awfully, Marmalade."

"Well, don't tell anyone about my great kindness. I only married your fa so I could become an extremely wicked stepmother."

"The wickedest of the wicked!" Sylvia screamed, and then

they both let out dramatic witch cackles as she left the room.

I slipped away down the servants' staircase and into the kitchen.

"Where are you off to?" Cook smiled.

"Oh, you know, a bit of shopping and maybe a trip back home."

The lie stung me a bit, as Cook was so kind. I put my gloves on and strode into the square where Agapantha and Sylvia were waiting. "I'll catch you up." I smiled. I couldn't risk anyone on the staff seeing Agapantha or Syliva speak to me, so I let them get ahead and walked behind them until the house was in the distance. 144

Agapantha turned and tipped her hat at me as she smiled. Her hair was slicked back and tucked underneath. "Do you know, Calypso, it is so fun not having to wear stockings. And look." She held her hands out. "No boring handbag. Everything is in my pockets. And I don't need a pocket mirror because no one expects me to look presentable at all!"

"If I hadn't seen you upstairs, I would never have recognized you. I daresay you would fool your mother."

Agapantha hooted. "I know. But we need to test it. We need to see if it's worked."

"Why don't you buy an apple at the fruit stall on the corner?" I said. We all sped up until we were running across the park. When we got to the stall, breathless, Agapantha pulled a ha'penny out of her pocket and strode over to Mr. Frencham's fruit stall.

"Three apples, please," she said, in a low and gruff voice.

We all waited for him to realize. I could feel butterflies in my stomach, and Sylvia was fidgeting next to me, her huge eyes fixed on Mr. Frencham. He smiled his usual smile and put the apples in a brown paper bag. Agapantha handed him a ha'penny.

"Have a good day, son," he said, and that was it.

"Mind how you go, son!" Sylvia hissed as we walked across Piccadilly. She was literally jumping up and down. "Mind how you go, son!" She clapped her hands. "You've done it, Panth!"

"I actually think it's partly you, working as a silent decoy," I said to Sylvia. "I mean, everyone is staring at your coat. A woman almost walked into a lamppost, she was so scandalized by it."

"Well, there you are," Sylvia said. "Perhaps we should start a life of crime. I could distract people with ornate coats, and Panth could pounce on their diamonds."

"And what would I do?" I asked.

"You would have to make the disguises and also probably be the brains of the operation." Agapantha took a huge bite of her apple. "See how I'm just eating away at this apple? Mother says ladies should never eat in public. I mean, I could go anywhere right now and no one would say a word. I could climb that tree without getting my skirt caught or being told off for being unladylike. I could buy a bicycle from Harrods and ride it right through the park. I feel like everyone looks at you differently, or more they don't even notice you. You can do whatever you like because no one cares."

We talked of all the things we could do if we all disguised ourselves as boys. Go to lectures at the university, stay out after dark, get the train to the seaside and paddle with our trousers rolled up. The more we talked about it, the more incensed we became, and the more I understood why Agapantha wanted to escape.

"I'm going to sew pockets into all my clothes as soon as I get home," Sylvia said. "I'm not ever carrying a silly handbag again. Or wearing stockings. Mine are so itchy, I hate them."

"Mother would disown me if I wore my legs bare," Agapantha said.

"I think she's more likely to disown you when you leave your very own coming-out ball and run away to the Amazon. I should think that will bother her more, Panth."

We pealed into laughter as we arrived at the army and navy stores. Sylvia and I waited outside and peered through the window at Agapantha. We watched her fool the man behind the counter as she bought a safari helmet, compass, water bottle, mosquito net, and penknife.

"Do you really think she'll do it, when it comes time?" I asked Sylvia as we watched her striding around with a hiking stick.

"I don't know. If she even gets as far as wearing trousers to her debutante ball, she will have done something braver than any girl who was presented this year. More than most girls, I should think."

I wondered if Sylvia ever considered how brave I was being even standing here talking to her in the street. Imagine if Mrs. Piercy or Mr. Corbet had decided to come to town.

Agapantha came out, swinging her bag of explorer's equipment. "He utterly believed me!"

The whole day was becoming more momentous than I had ever thought. Watching Agapantha get what she wanted just made me want to be more daring and get what I wanted too.

We rode at the front of the bus, Agapantha and Sylvia breathless with the freedom and the adventure of a day out in London, with no governess or chaperone to spoil things. It made me think of Dot and Gladys and Mary, how they went up to London on their days off. They wouldn't think of getting on the bus as an adventure. They would kill for a room full of pink taffeta frocks, and yet here were Agapantha and Sylvia, cock-a-hoop about being on the Number 33 to Petticoat Lane. The bus conductor didn't even look up as Agapantha bought tickets, but said, "Lucky fella, being out with two ladies. One on each arm," which made Sylvia dissolve into giggles until we were well past Tottenham Court Road.

I knew exactly where the warehouse was. Dad had gone there to buy rolls of fabric many times while I waited outside with the horse. Mr. Constantine's was famous all over the country. People came from Manchester and Exeter and Glasgow just to buy from him. Dad said he had been everywhere— China for silks and India for brocade and Italy for the very best leathers.

"We need to get off here," I said.

But I felt strange, as if the shadows of my past were casting off the buildings and over me. Pretending to be someone else felt more real here, so close to home. It felt as if Ma or Pa might walk around the corner at any moment. But I was here with Sylvia, in a place she didn't belong. I had managed to keep everything separate in my mind, and now it was all colliding.

"Are you quite all right?" asked Sylvia as we got off the bus.

I said yes but felt a lump in my throat, and I could feel tears stinging to come through. I felt frightened about everything suddenly and wished more than ever that I hadn't agreed to pretend to be Calypso.

"Gosh, Myr—Calypso, what is it?" Sylvia's eyes had grown huge. If it had been just Sylvia there, I would have spoken. I would have told her how strange it felt to walk straight into a place that belonged to a different time and to a life you could no longer claim as yours.

"Calypso?" Agapantha was genuinely concerned. "Are you well? Perhaps it's diphtheria, striking you down. That's why I'm never allowed out past the Ritz."

"Don't be a clod," Sylvia said. "It wouldn't take hold of her in the course of three minutes."

I walked around the corner and there it was: the imposing sight of Mr. Constantine's, a vast gray-walled building with a huge iron gate at the front.

"Crikey!" Agapantha let out a long, low whistle and then

a mischievous giggle. "Mother says girls oughtn't to whistle."

"It looks like a prison!" exclaimed Sylvia. "We had better get our story straight. So, I am a French woman. Panth, you are an English man. And Calypso is . . . Calypso."

She looped an arm through each of ours, and we all looked up at the factory.

"Well, I must say, I am giddy as a fish," Sylvia declared.

The warehouse trip had been my idea, but all of a sudden, staring up at the door, I doubted it. But it was too late.

Sylvia took a giant step forward and knocked on the door.

18

COMRADES

Sylvia

I was almost looking forward to a man like a jailer in a Dickens novel opening the door, all fat and stoat-eyed and devastatingly evil. I mean, why have a fabric shop that looks like a prison if you are not going to use it to full effect? I thought it was very witty to plan your exterior décor to match your personal level of wickedness. At least people knew where they were then. Think of the witch's house in fairy stories with fences made out of bones. It really tells people what sort of party-thrower you are before they knock on the door.

I don't actually know any French women, but I have seen the portrait of Marie Antoinette in the National Gallery with Smurf quite a few times. Just as I was trying to rearrange my face to a look of distant pondering crossed with duck à l'orange, the door opened. I started to introduce myself as Madame Gigi, but then I couldn't remember how to do a French accent. Usually I shout *boulangerie* a few times to get myself going, but that would make everything even more suspicious. And it was not Mr. Stoat-Eyes, as expected, but a boy about our age. His eyes registered me and my coat, and then Agapantha in her suit, and then Myrtle . . . and then he broke into an enormous smile.

"Myrtle!" he blurted out.

Myrtle shook her head at him pleadingly, but he didn't read the desperate signs for him to stop.

"Myrtle, what are you doing here? I'm pleased to see you." He looked at Panth. "That's the tweed I sent you. You've done a brilliant job—it looks cracking."

Agapantha chortled. "Gosh, you must have a doppelgänger. May I introduce Lady Calypso Mort—" But before she got to the end of the sentence, she saw Myrtle's quivering lips and trailed off. All the color and strength had drained from Myrtle's cheeks, and she suddenly looked much younger.

"I say, what on earth is going on?" Agapantha addressed the question directly to Myrtle, but I jumped in. After all, Lady Calypso Mortimer had been my idea.

"The thing is, Panth, we simply didn't know what a first-rate comrade you were until recent times. I mean, you know what most of Delphine's chums are like. Albertine North is the most dreadful tattletale, and as for Lavinia Andrews . . . too, too treacherous. She tells her mama everything. We couldn't risk it."

"I'm so sorry." Myrtle looked directly at Agapantha. "We should never have deceived you. The truth is, Lady Calypso doesn't exist. My name is Myrtle." Myrtle curtsied to Agapantha. "I am Lady Sylvia's maid."

"I say!" Agapantha was goggling. "Are you really? How thrilling. And all this time you have been pretending to be Sylvia's cousin? How awfully daring of you."

"Myrtle secretly helped me make Delphine's dress, you see," I said. "So when you came and asked us to make your outfits, well, I couldn't do it without Myrtle, could I? So . . . Look, you mustn't be a traitor, you promise? If anyone found out, Myrtle could get in the most dreadful trouble. I would too, of course."

Agapantha looked hurt. "That's jolly unkind, I should say. We shook as comrades, and comrades we are." She held out her hand to Myrtle. "You are a wonderful dressmaker and a wonderful friend. I think the world is just rotten. I can't be what I am supposed to be without pretending, and now it seems you can't either. I don't think it's us that are wrong, everything else is. You have kept my secrets and so I vow to you, I shall keep yours."

Myrtle shook her hand, and then Agapantha hugged her too. "Honestly, Myrtle, I never had friends as good as you two. In fact, I haven't really had any friends at all. Not *true* ones like you are."

I smiled at Panth. "Don't you think it's jolly funny how good Myrtle is at being a lady when we are so dreadful at it?"

I had forgotten that Agapantha was dressed as a boy, but the look of surprise on the face of the boy who had answered the door made me suddenly remember.

Myrtle saw it too. "How rude of me," she said. "This is Stan Trent. I know him from home."

The boy was looking at Myrtle quizzically, but he kept smiling. "Welcome to Constantine's. I work here sometimes, to train me up a bit. Mr. Constantine is my uncle." He held his arm out to welcome us in. "This is the best costume supplier in England. Whatever you need, we've got it."

I reached into my pocket and took out the list of materials we needed for Agapantha's costume and a few bits for her running-away case too.

The room beyond was fairly small. It glowed with little pools of light coming from lamps covered in shades of all different fabrics, lighting up glimpses of black and gold wallpaper covered in sphinxes and pyramids. There was a large red velvet chaise longue at one end and a desk and chair at the other. A huge cabinet made up of hundreds of tiny drawers covered an entire wall, and each drawer was labeled: *pearls, peacock feathers, French rubies, Japanese shells, Indonesian fans*. There was a gramophone and next to it a pile of records, and beyond that a long artist's table and a dressmaker's dummy. Standing by a small gas stove in the corner was a man wearing a midblue silk dress suit with a dark blue and gold capelet over the top. He poured hot chocolate into a china teacup and observed us. He looked from Agapantha-the-boy in her bottle-green suit to beautiful Myrtle, elegant in her silk suit, to me in my embroidered coat. "Well, I think this afternoon is going to be more exciting than I thought." His eyes twinkled over my outfit. "You are a true visionary, mademoiselle." Ha! Even without the accent I had channeled the spirit of France!

"This is Myrtle," the boy, Stan, said. "My friend I was telling you about, and . . . her friends—"

"Periwinkle. How do you do?" Panth managed.

"Sylvia Cartwright," I said before I could stop myself. What a dashed fool.

Mr. Constantine bowed to Myrtle first. "Delighted to make your acquaintance. My nephew has told me about you." And then he bowed to Panth and me too, and turned and clapped his hands. "Everything everybody needs is at Mr. Constantine's, but first, let us drink hot chocolate and look at your design."

He poured the hot chocolate from a jug with a gold parrot on it into bright green teacups with gold rims. He beckoned to us to sit down. "So, my favorite part. What are you creating?"

I pulled our design book out of my bag and turned the pages gently until I got to the right one. Mr. Constantine took the book and laid it on the artist's table. He ran his fingers around the edges of the design slowly.

"Who designed this?"

Myrtle and I looked at each other. "We both did," I said. "I designed the costume. It's for the debutante ball at Aspley House Thursday next."

Myrtle walked over and stood by the table. "I made these modifications." She pointed at some amendments on the page. "And I will cut the pattern and make it."

Mr. Constantine smiled.

"I have not seen talent like this for a long time." He ran his finger over the trousers on the page and looked at us both. "These will be controversial but *sensational*. I think they will be on every society page of every newspaper. I cannot wait."

He did a little jig on the spot. "Magnificent." He turned a page over in a book, picked up a pen, dipped it in an inkwell, and began to write very quickly. "Only Japanese silk will do." He looked at Stan. "Take it from the fifth aisle at the top."

His eyes scanned the design again and again and he started to sway elaborately to the tango music as he spoke. "Large sequins will reflect the light but not move with the fabric." He slammed his hands down on the desk and looked at Myrtle. "The shells will be hard, but it is not impossible."

He walked over to his cabinet and started to rummage through drawers. "I have gold iridescent paint you can brush onto each shell. Then, as she moves, she will shimmer." He found the pot and laid it down next to the design. He stopped talking and wrote more and more on his list.

"Gosh! I've never seen purple ink before," I said.

Mr. Constantine did a twirl. "There are many, many things here you have not seen before." He tore the list off his pad and held it out to the boy. "Take Miss Myrtle, the pattern-maker extraordinaire, to the warehouse and help her choose her tools." Stan took the list. And I noticed Myrtle was blushing.

19

FRIEND OR FOE?

Myrtle

The warehouse was the most amazing place I had ever been, a huge rectangular room with hundreds of shelves built right up to the roof. The ladders that dotted each row were so tall you couldn't possibly see the fabrics at the top. It felt like we were walking through a valley in a fairy story, with great mountains dwarfing us to either side. We were the only people there, and our footsteps echoed on the concrete floor.

Stan collected things on the list from the various shelves, but he wasn't his usual, chirpy, talkative self. He stopped by a ladder and began to climb it, list in hand. He reached for a box and peered into it.

"What sequins do you want again?"

"Turquoise. Some big and some small. I mean, what shape are the ones there?"

He leaned over and pulled out another box, shaking it to see what was inside. The ladder swayed slightly as he moved, so I held my hands out to steady it. He rattled the box again, and the sound reverberated around the room.

"There are no turquoise ones," he shouted down.

"They're probably in the box just along that says *blues*," I called up to him.

I saw him look from side to side as if making sure no one was coming, and then he looked down at me.

"Myrtle, what's going on? I mean, why is that girl wearing the tweed suit? Who is she?"

I would have to tell him now. I didn't have a choice. "I didn't want . . ." I realized I was still speaking in my put-on Calypso voice and felt silly and stopped. "Stan, I have been making clothes for that girl."

"I know that, Myrtle. I have a pair of eyes, you know. I've been helping you, sending you the fabric and everything."

He was right, he had been helping me, and now I felt like I had betrayed him somehow, not giving him the full story. "I didn't tell you because I didn't want you to get in any trouble."

His big eyes gazed down at me, full of worry and concern.

"Her name is Agapantha Portland-Prince. She is the duke of Wellington's niece. Next weekend she is going to run away . . ." Stan started to shake his head, as if he couldn't believe what he was hearing. I didn't want to go on. "Stan, she's running away . . . to the Amazon."

He spun around and the ladder shook. "*What?* You can't be serious!"

His mouth gaped for a second, and then he shook his head and carried on looking through the boxes.

"She's paying me, Stan, to make the clothes she needs."

His knuckles tightened on the ladder, and his face became very still. I had never heard him speak in the voice he used, quiet but deadly serious. "Myrtle, what were you thinking?" He looked almost desperate. "You've got to get out of this. This is bad."

"It's just making clothes, Stan. I'm not breaking any laws."

"If they come looking for her and find out you had a hand in it, you'll be done for."

My hands started shaking. Stan was just saying everything that deep down I had always been frightened of too. I dug my nails into my arm to stop from crying and keep my voice steady. "Stan, I've made the clothes now. Agapantha will pay me, and then it will be over. I know it sounds dangerous, but honestly, Lady Sylvia is my friend. She won't let anything bad happen to me. She's *helping* me. We're helping each other. She wants to be a dressmaker too. Stan, this is my chance—"

"Don't be such a fool, Myrtle. Come on, think about it. The duke of Wellington's niece *running away*. It'll be in all the newspapers, and who do you think they're gonna call when they wake up and find their precious darling *missing*? The *police*, that's who. And how long will it be before they come knocking on your door? Don't kid yourself about that Lady Sylvia; she'll turn on you in as quick as a flash. Myrtle, she ain't your friend. Friends understand each other—are you really telling me she understands what it's like for people like us? She's just using you because she's bored. You are a maid, and they are fancy ladies. It'll be you who ends up getting it. It's always us who ends up getting it."

"Why are you being like this? You said you wanted to help me. That we would help each other." The words started to sound jagged and teary.

"I'm *trying* to help you. Can't you see that? Back out now; get as far away from this as you can. *Don't* take any money off 'er. And what do you think your ma would have to say about all this? Bet you haven't mentioned it. I've a mind to find out her address and write to her."

The tears that were threatening to overwhelm me gave way to anger. I took my hands off his ladder, pulled another one up alongside it, and began to climb.

"You're not allowed up here!" he shouted. "It's dangerous."

"Says who?" I reached the top easily. He was right next to me. We both clung to our top rungs. I reached over for the blue sequin box, and Stan steadied my ladder. I glared at him as I showed him the sequins inside.

"You've got a nerve, *threatening* me, Stan. Don't you dare tell Ma or *anyone*. This is none of your business."

"Oh, none of my business, except when you need canvas and tweed and suit lining and green cotton, funny that. All I'm saying is that you should think about your ma."

"I *am* thinking about her!" I shouted. "I never *stop* thinking about her. That's why I'm doing all this, for *her*. So, one day I can bring her back to Stepney, buy her a tailor's shop, make her happy."

My face was burning, and I was biting the inside of my mouth to stop tears from spilling out. Stan just looked wounded and confused, as if he wasn't quite sure how this had happened between us. "I won't write to your ma, Myrtle, course I won't. I'm just frightened for you. You ain't one of them, you don't have pots of money and fancy parents to protect you. You ain't special."

Neither of us spoke, but the energy of the anger and hurt and fear between us was so powerful, it almost felt like we were still shouting at each other.

"I don't think I'm special. I know I'm not. Special people don't have the things they want taken away from them, their family and their home and the things they love to do. I just want to be something more than a maid, Stan. Just like you want to be an actor. You might never become one, but doesn't it make you feel good to *dream*?"

He looked for a moment like he might cry, but then he climbed back down the ladder. I held the box in one hand and stepped down slowly.

"Stan, you don't have to have anything more to do with this. I won't ask you for anything else, I promise."

I picked up my pace, but my dress got caught on a jutting nail. I tried to hold the box as well as the ladder with one hand so I could unhook it.

"Wait! I can help you." Stan stepped onto my ladder.

"I'm fine." But as I said that, my dress ripped and I fell, the box of sequins falling onto the floor and making a sound like a waterfall hitting rocks. I had fallen directly onto Stan. We both lay on the floor for a second, in shock. All the air had been knocked out of me, and I couldn't make any sound, couldn't make my stomach draw in breath.

"Are you all right?" he asked anxiously.

I stood up and finally took a huge gulp of air. "Yes." I turned from him, holding the split in my dress together with one hand, and walked back down the aisle toward the velvet curtain.

"All I'm saying," Stan said, "is that Sylvia can never really be your friend, because she'll never get it, what it's like to have dreams you can't make come true. She already lives in a dream world. Look, Myrtle, I just can't bear the thought of you getting into trouble. But I'll leave you alone if that's what you want."

We made our way back to the others, neither of us saying a word, and came in to loud Charleston music and Mr. Constantine shouting, "Forward, forward, backward, backward! Charleston, Charleston! Anybody can Charleston!" He sang and threw his arms in the air, swishing back and forth as Agapantha and Sylvia copied him.

They all looked up at us. "Come and dance. It's a *dream!*" Sylvia shouted, without a single care in the world.

20

DOOMED

Sylvia

Agapantha burst into the room before Corbet could even announce her. She hurtled past him and straight into me. Even at the best of times, Agapantha is like a baby hippo—she doesn't really know her own strength—so when she hoofed herself right at me, I didn't stand a chance.

Corbet's face did not move. He merely watched us disentangle ourselves from each other on the rug.

"Gosh, Panth, good thing the fire wasn't lit, or we'd both be toast. Corbet, be a comrade and ask Cook to send up a real feast. Lady Portland-Prince is clearly in some sort of hysterical fervor. If there are lemon curd sandwiches, all the better, and also perhaps hot chocolate and jam tarts. Jam tarts are jolly good for hysterical fervors."

Corbet bowed his head as if he perfectly understood. "Cook is just making up the tea things now, Lady Sylvia." And then he left.

"Panth! What's happened? Have you been contacted by a spirit from beyond the grave? That's happening in the book

I'm reading at the moment, best thing for that is a pure soul and gar—"

"Sylvia, the most awful thing has happened." She looked absolutely bereft, like her world had ended.

"Have they found out about Periwinkle Smith?"

She shook her head. "It's just the most awful, awful luck."

And then there was a sharp knock, and Myrtle came in carrying a huge tray of tea. She shut the door quickly. "I said I'd take the tray up, because I knew you weren't due today, so I—"

"The whole thing's off," Panth said. I thought she was going to cry, but instead she kicked the coal scuttle extremely hard and made a giant dent in it. "All off! Everything. I can't go."

Myrtle put the tray down. "Have your parents found out?"

"No, nothing like that." She pulled a piece of paper out of her pocket and waved it at us. "The ship isn't sailing on the twenty-eighth anymore. Something about the spring swells in the Pacific. It's leaving on the twenty-seventh at three a.m., with the first tide."

"The night of your ball," Myrtle said, and put her hand very gently on Agapantha's shoulder. "That really is bad luck, I'm sorry."

"But . . ." I couldn't believe it. Agapantha's escape. Her wardrobe of men's clothes. Her dream. "Surely there's another expedition. Is there another . . ."

Agapantha shook her head. "This was my one chance. I

know it was. I could only cope with doing the beastly season because I knew I wouldn't be there for the end of it. Every time Mummy talks about the debs' delights and asks who I danced with, I laugh on the inside because I know I shan't be marrying any of them."

"Could you leave in the daytime, before the ball?" Not even I had the heart to eat now.

Agapantha shook her head. "I've thought about it a hundred times. Mummy has turned the whole house into Mount Olympus. Everything is gold, and the lake is even going to be filled with synchronized swimmers dressed as mermaids. I simply can't do it to her. She's terribly sweet; she can't help it that she got the wrong daughter. But even if I wanted to, I won't be left alone the whole day. I wouldn't be able to escape if I tried."

We all climbed into the gondola and lay on the bottom of it. It swayed from side to side very gently and no one spoke. There was nothing to say. Everything we had worked for had been taken away from us in a flash. It would all just become some silly game we played the year of Delphine's debutante season. Agapantha wouldn't wear our costume—she had told us she couldn't because she wasn't leaving triumphantly. She was staying, and her mother would scold her heartily for deceiving her about it. I wouldn't get to see my costume come to life, wouldn't get to see it in all the papers. I thought it would be the first step toward Myrtle and me becoming dressmakers to the stars. But now that thought felt childish and ridiculous. A stupid fantasy.

Myrtle spoke into the air above her. "How long would it take you to walk to the docks? If you left your ball and went straight there, I mean? Could you get there?"

"Four hours at least, I should think, but how would I take my suitcase? I'm sure the one time in my whole life I couldn't slip out unnoticed is from my own debutante ball."

I jolted up. "Myrtle's got it. There must be a way. Think, we all need to *think*."

I clambered down and scooped all the tea up into the tablecloth, but then quite unexpectedly there was a knock at the door, and Mrs. Piercy walked in. Before I could stop myself I gasped loudly and looked straight at the gondola. You could still see it rocking, but only Agapantha was visible.

"Hullo," Panth said jollily, and waved to Mrs. Piercy.

"Good afternoon, Lady Portland-Prince," Mrs. Piercy said politely. "The duchess would love for you to join us for dinner this evening if you are not engaged elsewhere?"

"Most certainly am not, and your cook always does such crackerjack desserts."

"Cook will be delighted to know you think so." And then she was gone.

Panth and I immediately descended into hysterics, but Myrtle didn't join in.

"It's not funny," she said, sitting up in the gondola. "It's my *job*. Mrs. Piercy is my boss. She could sack me."

"Oh, Mrs. Piercy's a good egg, really. Come on, Myrtle, don't be so dramatic. She didn't see you anyway." I climbed back up and offered her a sandwich, but she shook her head.

Agapantha took three jam tarts and I ate five scones, but we still couldn't come up with anything.

"How many people are going to the ball?" Myrtle asked. I could see she was thinking intently.

"Five hundred." Agapantha groaned. "Can you *imagine*?"

Myrtle was calculating. "And that's before staff and the mermaids and the band. There'll probably be a thousand people there, all told."

"I know, hideous." Agapantha sighed.

Myrtle sat up. "Don't you see? There are so many people that if you got lost momentarily, it would be hard to find you."

"Yes! *Of course*. Panth, you just need to go to the ball, have your entrance with your pa and all that, say hullo to the queen or whoever, and then make a dash for it."

Agapantha was up too, and the boat rocked wildly. "But what about getting changed and my suitcase and everything? And how would I know the way?"

"Myrtle and I will come. We can come in disguise. We can help create a diversion, and then get you changed and out of the house."

"There is no way I am coming, Sylvia." Myrtle cut dead through me with a forcefulness I had never heard before. "It's too risky."

Something about the seriousness of her tone let me know she would not negotiate.

I shrugged. "Suit yourself, although I think you're being

desperately silly. No one would know who you are. It's far more dangerous for *me*. I might get recognized and then be in fearful trouble. I'd be sent to some prison of a boarding school at the very least. You will miss a terrific party, and seeing Panth escape."

"I don't mind," Myrtle shot back. "I will do everything I can to help from here."

Agapantha and I both nodded.

"I just need a way to get from the ball to the ship." Agapantha sighed. "I don't think there will be time on foot. What I need is . . ."

And at exactly the same time we all said exactly the same thing: "A horse."

21

YELLOW ROSES FOR FRIENDSHIP

Myrtle

Every night after Dot and Mary and Gladys had fallen asleep, I made my way up to the attic to work on Agapantha's costume. Usually I felt most at peace when I was sewing, but since the day at the warehouse, nothing was working. The silk for Agapantha's trousers was slippery and wouldn't hold when I tried to cut it. My needles kept snapping in the machine, and my seams didn't sit straight. There was an uneasiness inside me that I tried to push down so I could keep going, but it wouldn't leave me be.

Mrs. Piercy gave me my wages in their little brown envelope. "You look tired, Myrtle dear."

"I'm not sleeping that well, Mrs. Piercy." Not sleeping at all was the truth of it, because even when I did manage to sneak back down from the attic to bed, worries about Agapantha's escape and guilt about the argument with Stan stopped me from drifting off.

"Hot milk before bed tonight then, and a little lavender on

your pillow." Mrs. Piercy smiled kindly. "You have a lovely day off, now."

I hand-stitched the sequins on Agapantha's trousers the whole way across London, barely looking up, and I deliberately avoided the market when I got home. There was only one reason I had come.

I pushed the shop door open and watched Stan serving a customer. The place was still a jumble of fabrics and orders, but he seemed more in control than last time. He handed the lady her shopping and said good day and then looked up to serve me.

"Oh."

I looked back at the door. "Can I close it, just for a minute?"

He didn't respond, but I walked over and flipped the sign on the door from *Open* to *Closed* anyway.

I took the tiny package out of my pocket and held it out to him. "A peace offering," I said. "You don't have to accept it."

"Can I decide if I accept it when I know what it is?"

I handed it to him and watched him untie the string. He took out the handkerchief and looked at it. It had taken me a few hours I didn't have to embroider the roses and his initials. "Yellow roses symbolize friendship," I said. "I'm so sorry, Stan. I really do want to be your friend."

"It's odd that you've come here to say sorry," Stan said. "Because I wanted to tell you that I was sorry too." He looked at the handkerchief. "It's really something, Myrtle, thank you."

He took a breath. "I keep thinking about when I said you weren't special. Myrtle, *nothing* is a bigger lie than that. I am in awe of how special you are. It scares me . . . probably because it reminds me that I'm not. Myrtle, you are going to be someone, I know you are. I was just frightened for you. I don't trust those posh people to look out for you. But maybe I'm wrong."

"Sylvia didn't make me do any of it, Stan, that's the thing. I wish you could see them all, the duke and the duchess and Sylvia and her sister. They don't care what people think of them. They say what they want and do what they want, and they don't worry about what will happen to them. They just go on until they're stopped. And that's the thing—no one ever stops them."

"But there are different rules for us. We can't carry on like that."

"Well, maybe we should, just for a bit. Maybe if we carry on like them, we'll end up being able to do what we want just like them. I *want* to help Agapantha escape. Why *shouldn't* she? Stan, you said you would help *me* any way you could— well, that's how I feel about her."

He nodded. "So do you think she'll really go ahead and run away? The duke of Wellington's niece? To the *Amazon*?"

"I think she's got a fighting chance. I reckon we all do—as long as we're up for the battle, I think we can win."

"Funny sort of war, that you go dressed up in sequins and pearls to. Not like the one our dads fought."

"Well, we're fighting for different things this time." I saluted like a solider. "Just fighting to be whatever we want to be. Explorers, actors . . ."

He saluted back. "Famous fancy fashion designers."

"Exactly."

"So, how *is* she gonna escape?"

We had been over the plan a thousand times. We had lain in the gondola and thought of every last detail. But now, Stan asking me to say it out loud made me doubt it somehow. "Sylvia is going to go to Agapantha's debutante ball in disguise. She will wear a mask so no one will suspect who she is. It's a costume ball, so it won't seem odd at all. She will be announced as Lady Hero Fairfax. Agapantha has added her to the guest list. She told her ma that Hero had learned ballet with her when she was small, and her ma didn't think anything of it."

Stan chuckled. "Hero Fairfax."

"Honestly, they're all called the silliest things. Anyway, Agapantha's bag will be packed and ready, and then Sylvia will make sure she can slip away just after midnight. She'll help her get changed and leave the house without anyone seeing."

"But where's she got to get to, if she even makes it out, I mean?"

"The docks."

Stan shook his head. "That's miles! On foot it would take hours. And that ain't a part of town you want to be getting lost in. And she will get lost, I reckon. Even I don't go down the docks at night."

"Well, she can hardly try to hail a taxi—it would draw far too much attention. She can't risk it."

"She probably wouldn't make it on foot anyway. No one's that fast."

"She might. She's drawn a map; it is almost possible. And there isn't another option—she's got to try. We've thought of a thousand ways to take a horse from the stables, but the grooms would catch them."

A lady knocked on the door. "We're closed," Stan shouted, and she huffed away. "I'll do it." He looked excited. "Spots ain't exactly a racehorse, but she ain't a snail neither. She'd get her there. And I know the way."

"What? Stan, you didn't want *me* mixed up in it when you found out, and now you're all for it? Don't be daft. If you're caught—"

"Listen, I want to do it. To help you and because I think you're right. I just wasn't as brave as you. That's what I've been thinking all week. I want to have your courage, Myrtle. And we're friends." He held up the handkerchief. "Proper friends. If you're mixed up, I wanna be mixed up too."

"Do you mean it, Stan? You'll really do it?"

"Yes, I will. And anyway, I want to go to this ball. Tell that Agapantha she can give me a froufrou name and I'll come as well. It'll be my first proper acting role. I'll make myself a right fancy costume too. I mean, a posh ball in London? Now, that is gonna be something."

It stung a bit, the thought of Sylvia and Stan both getting to see Agapantha at the ball and me being stuck at home like Cinderella. But, if that was what it would take to get Agapantha her dream, I'd do it. "Thank you, Stan. Really and truly, thank you." I looked around the shop and suddenly felt really pleased that it was him standing behind the counter where I used to be. "Good thing you've learned all those dances, then?"

"Too right." He spun around on the spot. "I can fox-trot now and waltz and Charleston."

"Charleston." I burst out laughing. "*Charleston!* Not you too! Is there a lot of call for that in Stepney?"

"Come on, dance with me. I'll show you."

I shook my head and turned the sign back around to *Open*. "One day maybe, but not today. I've got work to do."

I ran down the street and jumped on the bus just as it was leaving. I waved to Stan at the shop door and he waved his handkerchief back. When I saw him again it would be after the night of the ball. Stan was the missing part of the plan, and I had found him.

22

IRIS AND HECATE

Sylvia

"Of course, I *could* go without you. But I simply don't want to. Not coming is not very comrade-like, I must say. I mean, you wouldn't be doing anything illegal, or even terribly naughty, really. You've simply been invited to a ball. You're acting as if someone has asked you to eat rotten snails. Agapantha *needs* us, and we can't let her down. What if the whole plan failed because we hadn't been there?"

Myrtle didn't take her eyes off the shell she was painting. She brushed it with a stroke of gold and then picked up another one and did the same, laying them out carefully in front of her in a row.

"Myrtle, do come on. I would do it alone, I would, but it would be much more fun together. And besides, you are somewhat the brains of this operation. You know how I get distracted by top-notch pastries and such. If you are there, then Agapantha has a much better shot at getting away. I can be the distraction, but then you can help her get changed, get her suitcase, and get out."

"Sylvia, *I* want to come, of course I do. I think about it all the time. But it's just too risky."

Myrtle was being infuriatingly, pointlessly priggish. Of all the things to be a priss about, going to a ball was the silliest of all.

Myrtle laid another shell down on the row and brushed it in gold before speaking. "Sylvia, if *you* are found out, you will get in trouble with your father. If *I* am found out—"

"I will just explain to Marmalade and no one will care at all. It's just a party. Myrtle, you have made the most jaw-dropping debutante ball costume that London will have ever seen. Don't you want to be there for its big moment? And honestly, I think you being there could be the difference between Panth getting her dream and not. Don't you think we should really give it our all? We'd do the same for you."

Myrtle turned her back on me and looked out the window for a little while. "How will I even get the night off? What would I wear?"

I did a triumphant *whoop* and the gondola rocked. "You *are* going to come! I knew I would persuade you. I know you, and you simply wouldn't be asking what you would wear if you were not imagining coming. Think of it, Myrtle, you and me at a deb ball! We can hear what everyone says about Agapantha's costume. We will *all* be a part of the plan! Together! We will dance the Charleston! And there'll be topping snacks. Come on, let's practice again. How about a tango?" I climbed down a few rungs and jumped to the floor.

"Sylvia, it's one thirty in the morning," Myrtle hissed. "We don't have time for this." But she put her paintbrush down carefully and climbed after me.

"We can't put the gramophone on. It'll wake everyone," Myrtle whispered, but she held both my hands. "What shall we do?"

"A waltz." I straightened my back. "I will lead and then you can next."

We started to count together. "One two three, one two three. Round and back and down. One two three, one two three round and back and down."

"You are out of time," Myrtle said as I trod on her foot.

"How can I be out of time when there isn't any music?"

"I don't know." Myrtle laughed her soft laugh. "I didn't think it possible either, but apparently it is."

"Well, excuse me, Lady Calypso."

Myrtle quickened her step. "I'll lead." She was a fantastic dancer. And she knew lots of dances I had never heard of, too. Myrtle is thoroughly combobulated in every way and I am *most* the opposite. She reminds me of a perfectly iced sugar cookie. It is peculiar how sometimes people who are so opposite can in fact share strands inside themselves that are entirely the same. When Myrtle and I are working, it is as if our strands are completely intertwined and we are just one dressmaker. As if the dress we are making can only exist in between us both, in the space where we connect.

"What made you change your mind?"

Myrtle stopped dancing. "When we started doing this, I just wanted to carry on making clothes, to keep that part of me alive." Her voice became softer. "To keep my dad with me, I suppose, and then to save money to bring Ma over. But then when they put Lady Delphine's dress in *The Tatler*, I started to feel something different. Like maybe I could really buy the shop for Ma and even more than that. Lately, I've started to let myself dream that maybe we really can do it one day . . . become couture dressmakers. Going to the ball feels like saying out loud we can do it."

"Do you know, that's precisely how I feel too." I grabbed her hand and pulled her over to the design book and opened it to the page after Agapantha's Poseidon costume. "What do you think?"

"I thought about what you said: you have to match the dress to the person. And don't you adore black? And aren't you the one who makes the magic? Who makes the designs come to life? You *had to be* Hecate the sorceress," I said.

Myrtle put her face closer to the page and looked at every detail.

"The embroidery will take me a long time," she said finally.

"Is *that* all you have to say?" She could be so sharp sometimes. She looked up and put her arms around me.

"Only a true friend could have made something that expresses me so well," she said. "Thank you. And what about you? Are you going in floor-length black too?"

"Not a chance." I flipped the page over and watched her react.

Hecate Costume

Destiny

Incantations

Zodiac

Divine Magic

Spells

Magic

embroidery

Myrtle gasped. "Sylvia! You will look like a film star."

"I know. That is exactly what I want to look like." I struck a pose in the mirror like Greta Garbo in *Torrent*.

Myrtle looked up at my bed. "You know, we probably have the fabrics here to make these, with the costumes in the attic and your dress-up box. If we finish Agapantha's tonight, we'll have time." Myrtle was always *thinking things through*. She just loved the detail. "Let's push on and do one more hour. Just finish the final row of sequins on the sleeve, and get the shells all painted, ready to drill holes through tomorrow."

Myrtle yawned one of her elegant yawns but went and sat in her sewing chair.

"And I have something else to show you." I dived through the curtains onto my bed and got the velvet box I had hidden there earlier. "Look!"

I undid the clasp and gently pried the lid open, picked the tiara up, and put it on my head. I stood up. "Gosh, it's awfully heavy. I hope poor Panth can bear it. Her neck might sink into her chest. I wonder how the queen can be bothered. It's like wearing a hat made of lead."

I walked slowly over to the mirror.

"It makes one walk in a stately fashion or it falls off. It's perfect, don't you think?"

Myrtle seemed completely awe-inspired, as if an archangel had appeared. "Did the duchess let you take it?"

"Dash, no. It's made of ginormous diamonds. A Russian empress gave it to some great-great-granny of hers."

Myrtle sprang up from her chair. "Sylvia, you must go and put it back. You *must*." She didn't even want to look at it. She turned around and paced to the window. "It must be worth an awful lot of money. More money than . . ."

"You know they print money at the bank, don't you? They just make it. And diamonds are just rocks, the same as pebbles on the beach. People just like them because they are prettier than pebbles, that's all."

"You are being deliberately stupid. We could get in so much trouble. We could be hanged." Her eyes were flashing, and she was shaking.

I burst out laughing. "It *belongs* to us. You can't be hanged for owning something."

"It doesn't belong to me, Sylvia. I can't believe you would involve me in something like that. It's stealing."

"It's borrowing, which is entirely different. We'll put it back the very next day."

"What will the duchess do if she finds out?"

"She simply won't find out. For a start, she won't even recognize it, all covered in shells and ribbons. And she's not even going to the ball, and by the time she wakes up the next day, we'll have put it back. It's too, too perfect for Poseidon's crown, don't you think? But we'll have to make a trident out of something."

"But what if she *does* find out?" Myrtle just wouldn't let it go.

I rolled my eyes. "Honestly, Myrtle. You do worry about the silliest things. I should think if Marmalade found out, she would positively roar with laughter, but she's not going to. It's as simple as that."

23

SECRETS AND SHELLS

Myrtle

The knocking sound wandered into my dream and got louder and louder.

"Myrtle?"

I was just coming round when Dot walked into the room.

"Myrtle, you missed dinner. Are you sick? Cook has saved you some, but she's awful worried."

I saw Dot glance over the room. There was fabric everywhere. I had gotten bolder the last few days, bringing pieces back to my room to work on. Silk and satin and sequins had managed to cover every single surface. She reached over and picked a sequin off my cheek and looked at it perched on the end of her finger. And then she saw the Poseidon tail, hanging over the edge of the sewing table. Her mouth hung open.

"Myrtle! What is all this?"

I didn't want to lie to Dot—she was my friend—but I didn't really have any choice. Seeing Lady Delphine crying in her Parisian gown, and offering to help her, seemed like a long time and a lot of lies ago. How would I even begin to describe it all to Dot? I picked up the trousers—I had sewn the very last shell to the hems and now they were finished. I held them up.

"What do you think?"

Dot shook her head. "I ain't never seen anything like it. Even at the pictures. What . . ." She seemed completely lost for words. "What is it?" she whispered, as if she were seeing a new species of animal for the first time.

"They're dress trousers. For a ball."

"Dress . . . *trousers*?" Dot looked at me and back at them. "Can I?"

"Course." She ran her fingers across the sequins, and they shimmered as she touched them.

"Myrtle Mathers, did you . . . make these?"

"Yes." Seeing the look on her face made me swell with pride.

"They are the most . . . I dunno what to say. Myrtle, they are just . . . they're heaven! Who are they for? Not Lady Sylvia?"

My heart started to beat a little faster, and I tried to make the lie form in my throat, but the way Dot was in awe of the costume made it hard not to tell her the truth. Why shouldn't she be part of it too? It didn't feel right to keep it from her when we spent every day washing pots side by side.

"Promise you won't tell anyone?"

Dot nodded, a little confused. "Yes."

"They are for Lady Delphine's friend, Lady Agapantha, for her debutante ball."

Dot's mouth was hanging open. "*You* are making *her* deb ball costume?" she gasped. "Myrtle, I don't believe it, I can't. It will be in the papers! You won't be a maid no more!"

"I haven't done it in work time," I assured her. "I've done it on my time off. She's going to pay me, Dot, and I'm going to save the money so I can buy my dad's tailor's shop back. One day, I'm gonna bring my ma back home."

"Wow." Dot smiled, but a weaker, more pretend smile. "Wish I could bring my ma home."

I reached out and touched her arm.

"You'll have a home of your own one day, Dot."

She shrugged. "Maybe."

A tiny wave of panic crept up me. Telling her might have been a terrible mistake. There was nothing to stop her going straight downstairs and telling them all over evening cocoa. "Listen, Dot, you can't tell anyone. I don't know if I'm allowed to work outside of being a maid. What would Mrs. Piercy say?"

"You'd get the boot, I reckon. She don't like people who think they're better than they ought to be. I mean, we're not even supposed to talk to them unless they tell us to."

Hearing her say it so matter-of-factly made me feel sick. I knew she was right. She could end everything now if she wanted to. She must have seen my face change.

"Don't worry, Myrtle, I ain't gonna tell no one. You're my mate, aren't you?"

I couldn't stop thinking about what she had said. The work wasn't even the worst of it. Pretending to be a grand lady. Working with Lady Sylvia. And now going to a debutante ball. Dot looked shocked enough by the trousers, let alone everything else. All the things Stan had said at the warehouse bubbled up, all the things I had been thinking all along too.

"Your secret is safe with me. I swear, Myrtle. If you're making money and getting out, good for you. Just don't forget who your friends are."

I smiled. "I promise." She reached her hand out and we shook on it.

Dot let out a low whistle. "Trousers. At a ball. Trousers! I ain't never heard the like. Is it even legal? But I suppose if you're posh, you can do what you like. But trousers . . . at a ball. Not even the duchess would do that."

It made me a bit nervous. What *would* people think? It was all starting to become very real indeed.

She smiled. "Are you coming for this cold dinner, then?"

I laid the costume back down. My hands stung and were red and raw. The needlework was making my fingers ache.

"Tell Cook I fell asleep, but that I'm coming now."

Dot walked to the door. "Can I keep this?" She held her finger out with the large aquamarine sequin on the end.

"Course you can."

"It'll remind me of you when you've left us all behind and you're serving customers in your own blinkin' shop!"

"That won't be for a while," I said. "But if I ever do, you could come and work with me."

After Dot had shut the door behind her, I opened my special tin. I had a lot of money now: all the money Lady Delphine had given me for doing her dress, and the bits and bobs the girls had given me for making things for them. Soon it would have the money from Agapantha in it too. It was more than I'd make in half a year as a maid. It would be enough to bring Ma home for a holiday, and enough to make buying the shop back for her more than just a dream—I would be part of the way there already.

Downstairs, I ate my dinner quickly and did my evening chores. I heard Agapantha being announced at the front door and Lady Cartwright talking to her.

"Agapantha, darling thing, how are the preparations for your ball? I wrote to your mama yesterday saying how excited Delphine is. I mean, Mount Olympus! So clever. The queen will be kicking herself that she didn't think of it for the summer ball at the palace."

The mention of Lady Delphine at the ball startled me. What would I do if she saw me? How would we explain it? New dangers kept cropping up and making me feel sick. It was a bad idea. I should have trusted my gut instinct from the start. I needed to explain to Sylvia that it was a mistake.

I took my apron off and went to collect the costume. I almost bumped into Mrs. Piercy, carrying a tray to Lord

Cartwright's study. My heart clenched, and I nearly ran to Lady Sylvia's room.

"Oh, you're here!" Agapantha threw her arms around me as I shut the door. "Now I know you're really a maid—you do seem a scream in that uniform with your little cap and everything. Can you believe it's only two days away?"

"Are you nervous?" I asked, because I myself was getting more nervous about everything by the second.

Agapantha's eyes met mine, and she spoke carefully.

"Not about the costume. Although no doubt Mummy will implode with the horrors. But the plan . . . yes, I am. I'm nervous about it going wrong, but nervous about it going right too."

"It won't go wrong." Sylvia's assuredness relaxed me. "We are going to be there for the first part, and Stan won't let us down for the second."

"Well, I hope not." Agapantha said. "I sent him the invitation. Well, I sent Mr. Lancelot Lecelles one and told him where to leave Spots. I just hope he got it and doesn't change his mind.

"Lancelot is *such* a good name for him, our knight in shining armor. He seems a frightfully good sort," Agapantha said. "He'll come through for us, I'm sure."

She took off her wool suit and stood in her drawers and camisole, taking a deep breath. We helped her into the underbodice first and then attached the overlay garment. Lady Sylvia and I both wore gloves so not a sequin, shell, or pearl could catch on anything. Then Agapantha stepped into the trousers, one leg at a time, and Sylvia and I buckled her royal blue satin shoes, each one adorned with the tiniest golden seashells. Agapantha turned to look at herself in the mirror.

"Wait!"

Sylvia ran over and picked up the black velvet box. Lady Cartwright's tiara was almost unrecognizable. Sylvia had transformed it into Poseidon's crown with gold shells, starfish, and long swaths of blue and green silk, hanging down in waves. Agapantha bowed slightly so Sylvia could place the crown on her head. It had taken whole nights of work to make the costume. And all that time I had imagined Agapantha wearing it: her particular gait, the way she moved, and the way she laughed. But I could never have been prepared for how breathtaking it looked in real life. We all just stood there, gazing at her and the way she looked in it.

"I'm not nervous anymore," Agapantha said as she admired herself.

Reflected in the mirror, we looked quite an odd trio. There was Agapantha, resplendent and strong; Sylvia, twinkling with mischief and energy in her grandmother's Regency nightgown; and me in my black dress. I ran my fingers over the needle and thread I had embroidered onto it that day at home. I had sewn my future without knowing it.

"I feel as if everything is about to change," Agapantha said.

"Because it is!" Sylvia and I said at exactly the same time.

24

RUNAWAYS

Sylvia

Myrtle knocked on my door at eight thirty, exactly as planned. I pulled her into the pitch-black of the room. I had drawn all the curtains so not a chink of the summer twilight could get through.

"I can't believe we're actually doing it," I hissed.

"How are we going to get dressed with the lights off?" she whispered back.

"We'll have to light a candle. Otherwise they will know I'm awake and haven't taken to my bed with a headache."

I heard Myrtle's gentle footsteps and a match strike, and then a tiny orb of warm light flickered. Her face came into view. Even now, she didn't look in the slightest giddy or tense. It was quite maddening, really.

"I must say, you're just like Mary Queen of Scots at her execution, not even a glimmer of nerves."

"I am nervous. I suppose when we're actually wearing our dresses, it might feel a bit more real. I feel as though I'm about to perform in a play."

"Well, you sort of *are*, as Calypso Mortimer."

"I know," she whispered into the dark. "Except we haven't even had a dress rehearsal."

The room had taken on an electric energy, as if the air knew something was afoot. I walked over and climbed the stairs to my bed. "Honestly, we shouldn't have hung them in there. All night I kept thinking there were two women at the end of my bed."

I had meant it as a joke, but neither of us laughed. I unhooked both of the dresses and brought them over.

"Have you ever worn anything without sleeves?"

She shook her head. "No. I feel like only grown-up women are allowed. Not that I've ever seen my ma, well, with her arms out."

We both smiled.

"It's quite daring of us, really. I almost forgot. I have something for you. I didn't buy them; they're Marmalade's."

I handed her the box. She opened it and picked up one of the shoes. They were black satin dancing slippers with diamond-encrusted heels.

"They'll match, won't they? I mean, you couldn't have worn your work shoes. It would have given the game away."

"I can't borrow Lady Cartwright's shoes! I can't, Sylvia. It would be awfully wrong. I mean, actually *wearing* the duchess's shoes!"

"She won't notice. She has hundreds of pairs of shoes. It's just for one night. You *can't* wear yours—they will draw attention."

As usual I couldn't tell what she was thinking.

"I suppose you're right."

We both stood holding our dresses on their hangers in front of us.

"Gosh, are we really, really going to do it?" I whispered into the half-light.

Even now, Myrtle was checking the embroidery on her dress. "I don't know. Even standing here with the dress in front of me I don't know. I can't see the future."

"I know what you mean. I can't even imagine us standing here, dressed in them."

"Well, maybe things only feel real when they actually happen to you."

Myrtle swished the dress in front of her.

"I imagined coming here so many times, and then when I got here, it was nothing like how I imagined. It was better in every single way. It's made me want so much more than I ever have before. And . . . when . . . when I tried to imagine my father dying . . ."

She paused. She paused for so long that I felt I ought to say something, to help her out of the silence, but at the same time, it felt like *her* silence, and it would be wrong for me to be the one to break it. I saw her whole face become incredibly still.

"I tried to imagine my father dying again and again, as if it would help when he actually did. But it was nothing like how I imagined. Nothing at all. I don't know. I can look at drawings of clothes and I can imagine them in my mind and then make them real. But I can't seem to do it with anything else."

I took a step toward her and threw my arms around her and hugged her as hard as I could. She lifted her arms to hug me in return, our dresses sandwiched between us.

"We don't have to do it if you don't want to," I said, and squeezed her hard before letting her go.

She took a deep breath.

"No, I want to. After all, it's not a very good story, is it? The ball you never went to? The life you didn't quite dare to lead?"

"True. And when you think about what Agapantha is doing, we're not doing anything very daring at all, really."

Myrtle walked behind the bed curtains, and when she reappeared, she was wearing the dress.

"Oh, my goodness. *Myrtle.*"

I actually had no idea what to say. She stood in front of the mirror and pinned her hair simply off her face. The black bias cut of her dress skimmed over her and trailed into a puddle that fell perfectly at her heels. She wasn't wearing any jewelry, because she didn't have any. It was just the black sheath dress and her unbelievable beauty. Her dark eyes flashed. The dress was powerful; it made her look tall and imposing.

"Gosh, I would believe you had magical powers. It's honestly amazing, Myrtle. I have never seen anyone look the way you do. You just need one more thing."

I climbed the ladder to the gondola and reached in and picked up her present. I had spent hours making it, whittling it out of wood, painting it black, and decorating it with black crystals, jet, and tiny black pearls. I had attached a loop through the top so she could slip it onto her wrist. I clambered down and handed it to her. She held it in her hand and then picked it up and pointed it at the mirror.

"A wand for Hecate," she said, and laughed. "For a very practical witch. Sylvia, it's beautiful. Thank you." She started to dance, and I could tell she was excited.

"And now it's your turn."

Myrtle had to stand on a chair to help me into my dress. The caped back with all its rainbow streamers needed to be arranged exactly, so they flowed as I moved. I slipped my feet into Delphine's purple dancing shoes and did up the diamante clasps. I passed Myrtle the box of hairpins and watched her as she carefully pinned my hair in sections, leaving a few loose tendrils at the front.

"Are you ready?" she asked.

Myrtle placed the headdress on my head. The golden stars sprayed out like a halo, and the costume jewels glinted, even in the semidarkness. The gold of the dress sparkled every time my body moved, even as I breathed. Myrtle looked over it with her keen eye, searching for imperfections, but she couldn't find any.

"Are you pleased?" I asked. "I am—it looks so much better than my drawing."

Myrtle beamed. "Yes. And I'm glad I split the bodice. It works. But most of all, I'm glad you designed it. It's magical. You're magical."

"One last thing."

I opened the drawer and took out Marmalade's lipstick. It was bright crimson red. I put it on and pursed my lips, and then Myrtle did the same. Even if someone had come into the room, I doubt they would have recognized us. It made me feel like I wasn't actually myself. As if I had fully changed into another, glamorous and thoroughly beautiful, being. We put on the floor-length velvet opera cloaks I had taken from the attic, picked up our masks, mine gold and hers black, and we were ready.

I blew out the candle, and we were in complete darkness again. "Quickly!" I said. "Once we're in the corridor, neither of us can speak. It's too dangerous." I took her hand, laced my fingers between hers, and held tight. "The servants' staircase will be quicker, but it's more risky. What if Mrs. Piercy and Cook are still awake?"

"I think we should run to the guest room, then," Myrtle said, "and out the main door. It's the most direct route."

"But what will we do if someone comes?"

"Run," Myrtle whispered. "We'll have to."

I opened the door. The hallway was completely silent, but the lights hadn't been switched off for the night. Marmalade and Fa were still in the drawing room. I ducked my head back in.

"Ready?" Something about Myrtle's eyes made me think she wasn't. I squeezed her hand. I felt like I would have to take the first step. "Do you want me to go for it? Do you trust me?"

"Yes."

I danced down the hallway on my tiptoes to make as little noise as possible. I kept hold of Myrtle's hand, and she scurried behind me. When we got to the top of the stairs, I leaned over. Dot and Mary were turning the lights out.

"What if they come up here?" I mouthed. But it was too late. Dot was coming. We dived into Marmalade's dressing room. In the dark, the smell of lilacs and starch hit me.

"I can imagine you marrying a man called Jack," Dot was saying. "I just see you with one, that's all."

And then their footsteps got quieter and disappeared.

"Now!" I whispered, and launched into the corridor and down the staircase three steps at a time.

"Is that you, darling Sylv?" I heard Marmalade shout, but I had already opened the door. We ran down the drive and into the darkness ahead.

"The park is over there!" Myrtle shouted.

We hurtled out of the gates and that was it. Nobody opened the door, nobody ran after us. The park was deserted. I was glad of the black cloaks, not for warmth but because they camouflaged us against the dark night.

"I have never been out alone at night! Never."

Myrtle's pace was quick. "Nor have I. Do you know the way?"

"Sort of. It's not very far. It's at Apsley House. The duke of Wellington is Panth's uncle, you see. But I'm not quite sure of my bearings."

I turned in one direction and then the other. All I could see was parkland, and the dark felt as if it were closing in. Every sound made me jump.

"Gosh, Myrtle. I didn't think about this bit."

"It's all right. We can work it out. Just let me think for a minute."

The moon appeared from behind some clouds and the park lit up.

"There's the pond," she said. "You said it's near the arch? So we need to go this way."

We had to go slowly to stop our shoes sinking into the mud, and Myrtle had to hold up the train of her dress to stop it from getting ruined. It took much longer than it ever seemed to in the day. But twenty minutes later, we found it. Hyde Park Corner came into view, and the lights of buses and restaurants twinkled. We emerged from a gate a little breathless, straightened each other's hair, and tried not to arouse suspicion, behaving as if it were perfectly normal to take a walk at night through Green Park in full Greek costume. We were the only ladies walking.

Apsley House was ablaze with torches. There were cars lined up all along the road, causing a traffic jam. Every time a car door opened, a deb would spill out, giggling and wanting to be noticed. There was a crowd of people gathered round, just watching people go in.

"There's Lavinia Andrews," I said. "She looks utterly ridiculous, as I could have predicted. Oh, she's come as a nymph.

Too, too boring. Oh, look! Albertine North has come as a sort of . . . what is that, even? Just a girl carrying a small harp? She's quite a good egg, though, really."

"How are we going to get in? They all have chaperones and are arriving in cars!"

I shrugged. "Well, we've jolly well got an invitation. It's none of their business *how* we got here. The point is, we have very much *arrived*."

I held my head up high and prepared to push through the throng of people, but I didn't have to—they just parted for us. Lots of gentlemen even took off their hats.

"Good evening," I said, "and good evening to you."

And then we were at the door. Light bulbs started flashing, and before I'd even had time to lift the mask up, I realized people were taking our photographs.

"Who are you, my darling?" a photographer shouted.

A footman opened the door for us without even asking to see our invitations. Another servant took our cloaks, and then we were ready. A line snaked up to the ballroom, and I could hear names being called.

"The duke and duchess of Northumberland. Lady Albertine North. Lady Amelia Bentley-Hooper and Mrs. Wetherington."

And then it was us. We both stepped through the door at the same time.

"Lady Hero Fairfax and Lady Calypso Mortimer."

25

FLASHBULBS AND FRILLS

Myrtle

The ballroom was already packed, and hundreds of people were dancing. The dresses were dazzling. So many rich colors, moving so quickly, made the whole room seem like a giant kaleidoscope. The lights hit the ladies' jewels, their diamonds and rubies and emeralds glittering as they spun and swayed. The ballroom was five times the size of the Cartwrights', and the band was five times bigger too. The stage was full of musicians, with a singer at the front in a peacock-blue suit.

We were at the top of the staircase, the entire ball below, waiting to be greeted by a line of people. It was too much to take in at once; I could have looked at the chandeliers alone for hours, watching them cast thousands of tiny rainbows across the costumed couples.

"What shall I say?" I whispered to Sylvia, but it was too late—we had reached the first person. I could tell it was Agapantha's mother. She had the same strength to her, the same huge blue eyes. Sylvia curtsied. I had never seen her do it before.

"Lady Portland-Prince." Sylvia let her mask slip for the slightest second while she greeted her.

"Oh, darling, you will have to remind me who you are. Girls your age, you know. It's the doe-eyed look in your eyes — I simply can't tell you apart."

"Lady Hero Fairfax." Sylvia was completely at home. Despite her anarchic *whoop*s and avant-garde sense of style, she knew what was expected of her. It was her world, after all. She understood the rules of it.

"Oh, of course! I do so adore the Highlands. I went there many times as a girl."

Lady Portland-Prince reached out and moved Sylvia's chin from side to side.

"You have a most excellent jawline—" She looked Sylvia up and down. "You must come to us for the hunt this winter."

And then all her attention was on me.

"Lady Portland-Prince," I said, trying to keep my voice steady. I curtsied the way Sylvia had, a short, not-too-reverent one. I moved my black lace mask to greet her. Her eyes wandered over my face and then up and down my whole body, as if she were searching for clues, trying to place me. She shook her head.

"So many of you, you know."

"Lady Calypso Mortimer," I said, and bowed my head ever so slightly.

"Mortimer?" She looked momentarily confused. "Oh yes, of *course*. Do send my regards to your dear mama, won't you?"

I smiled sweetly, imagining what my ma would think of Lady Portland-Prince's regards. And then she was on to the next person in the line, and we were in. I felt a knot in my stomach relax slightly.

As Sylvia moved down the staircase, everyone in the room looked up at her. Her headdress was sensational. She looked like a fairy queen, walking to her coronation. As she rounded the bottom of the staircase, the rainbow inserts in the cape detail of the dress splayed out behind her. It was breathtaking. Every girl in the room knew in that moment that they had lost the dress contest. Well, every girl except for one. I saw her on the other side of the room before she saw me. She was surrounded by other girls her own age, giggling and drinking champagne. I gasped a little to myself.

"Sylvia, look. Look at Agapantha!"

Sylvia looked up. "Her hair!"

Agapantha had cut all of her hair off. It was short—scandalously short. I had never seen a woman with hair like that, cut above her shoulders, let alone cut right close to the scalp like a man. She held Queenie in one hand and the trident we had made her in the other. She walked across the room to greet someone, and as she did, the girls behind us started talking.

"Trousers! Blanche, she really is wearing trousers, I promise you. Stand on that chair. Honestly, I have never seen anything like it. And all her hair is . . . gone!"

We heard some clamoring as the chair was climbed.

"Goodness!"

And then silence.

"Who would ever have thought it? Agapantha Portland-Prince. In trousers!"

"It is the most beautiful outfit I have ever seen. If I owned it, I would never take it off, not even for bed."

Sylvia and I exchanged a smile of pride. It had worked! Agapantha was wearing trousers to her debutante ball—the first girl to ever do so. And she was doing it in the most chic and daring fashion. The sequins rippled as she walked, and her crown, streaming with shells, was resplendent.

"We did it!" Sylvia shouted to me over the music. "We really, really did it!"

I couldn't stop looking at the clothes. At the mothers in their long, more old-fashioned gathered skirts and embroidered evening jackets. At the debs' delights in their evening attire, complete with top hat and tails. And all the debs. Lady Sylvia told me who they were all dressed as: sea nymphs and goddesses, Helens of Troy and sirens aplenty. There was a huge gold clock on the wall. It was eleven o'clock. If Stan didn't come, everything would be over before it had even begun. I closed my eyes and willed him to appear at the top of the staircase. What if he hadn't gotten the letter? What if he had changed his mind?

"We *must* dance!" Lady Sylvia dragged me toward the dance floor as a polka started up. A young man cut in and bowed to Sylvia.

"I know we haven't been formally introduced, but would you like to dance?"

Sylvia scrunched up her face. "Gosh, no, not really. I mean, I was rather hoping to not have to dance with anyone but myself."

He looked shocked and quite embarrassed.

"It's not you particularly. And anyway, I'm not very good at the whole being-led thing. Just ask Calypso."

Sylvia giggled and led me onto the dance floor. Everyone else was dancing in couples, but Sylvia danced by herself, her arms outstretched, her eyes closed, every inch of her enjoying how she felt in that moment. I wanted to be as free as her, but I didn't know how to be. And then Agapantha was with us.

She threw her arms around me.

"Honestly, Myrtle, everyone has been asking me who made my outfit. The lady from *The Tatler*, the lady from *Vogue*. When Mummy saw me, she went bright white and a maid had to bring her smelling salts. But now that the old *Tatler* says it's marvelous, she seems to have revived a bit. Everyone who has spoken to me has asked me!" She held my hand and squeezed it. "You could do it, you know, you and Sylvia. You really could. People are bonkers for your designs. Simply *bonkers*. You know Cecil Beaton is doing the photographs? He said mine was *the outfit of the decade*. We must get ours taken."

Agapantha reached out and grabbed Sylvia mid-flail.

"Come on, Sylv. We must get our photograph taken all together." And then she pulled us both into a huddle. "It's our only chance to commemorate this evening. The very, very best one of my life."

"Are you nervous?" I asked.

She shook her head. "No, I can't wait." She pointed to a door. "That's the one I told you about. Two flights up, and on the left is the bedroom with my things. My duffel bag and everything is ready. It's all under the bed."

I nodded. "I'll be there. As soon as I see Sylvia lead you away, I'll be there."

There was still no sign of Stan. Time was ticking by, and my nerves were starting to get the better of me.

We left the dance floor, and Agapantha led us up another staircase and into a grand drawing room where a photographer's studio had been set up.

Some girls in what now looked like completely ridiculous flounced skirts were having their picture taken. The photographer yawned a bored "thank you," and they gathered themselves up. As soon as he saw us, he came alive.

"These are *they*: the holy trinity of style." He bowed. "These clothes." He blew air kisses to our outfits. "These clothes are what my dreams are made of." He looked at me and then at Sylvia. "I must photograph you all together. I must."

I shook my head.

"Not me. I . . . I . . . can't. I . . . I really can't."

"She might later," Sylvia cut in. "She just isn't feeling awfully well at the moment. I will do it, but only in my mask."

The photographer narrowed his eyes quizzically before

going back to his camera. The backdrop had been made to look like Olympus, with bowls of fruit and classical paintings that no doubt belonged to the duke of Wellington. A chaise longue was laid out, and some props. I watched him arrange them both. Poseidon, holding Queenie, her head high, regal and imposing, standing astride, so her trousers were shown to full effect. And Iris, her array of colors dazzling, her crown and cape and golden mask.

I went to the window and looked down at the road below. People were still coming in, and crowds were still lining up to watch them. The moon was huge in the sky. I held my wand up and let the moonbeams sparkle over the jewels.

"Calypso?" The photographer called. I turned and the bulb flashed.

"Just one for me, darling." It was so quick, I didn't have time to stop him or to lift my mask to my face. It felt like things were swinging slightly out of my control.

As we walked back down the staircase, the clock came into view. "It's half past eleven," I whispered to Sylvia. "Do you know what you're going to do?"

She nodded. "Yes, I shall simply go and say there is the most terrific game of hide-and-seek going on in the gardens and that dear Agapantha must come immediately. And then I will just lead her away before anyone can say a thing about it."

I nodded, but inside I felt sick. It was all about to happen. We tried to look offhand, as if we were great friends catching up, but neither of us could stop looking at the clock, or

Agapantha, who was next to her parents, surrounded by people congratulating her on the magnificence of her ball.

As the clock struck quarter to twelve, Sylvia nodded at me. "At quarter past, I'll meet you where we came in. If all goes well, Agapantha and Stan will be gone by then—if he's here."

"He will be."

Sylvia disappeared into the crowd toward the Portland-Princes, and I was left quite on my own. From behind my lace mask, I felt totally safe and free to take it all in. I could see the queen and the princess Mary and dresses I had only seen in magazines before. I might never feel part of this world, but at this moment, I didn't feel less than it either.

I felt a tap on my shoulder and turned around. Looking older than he normally did, and in an evening suit with a golden laurel crown, was Stan. Before I could stop myself, I threw my arms around him. "You came, you really came."

We were both a bit taken aback by the hug. I felt myself blushing under my mask. "Of course I came. I said I would, didn't I? And besides, as if I'd miss *this*. I mean, *look* at it all."

We stood side by side, staring at the sheer wonder of the room before us, and then the band struck up a Charleston. Sylvia hadn't reached Agapantha yet. We had maybe five more minutes before we had to leave. Maybe the only five minutes Stan and I would ever be in a ballroom together for the rest of our lives.

"Come on." I held my hand out to him. "Would you like to dance?"

He shook his head jokily. "Waiting to do the asking, were you?"

"I said there wasn't a lot of call for it in Stepney. But we're not in Stepney now."

I took him by the hand and led him onto the ballroom floor. We stood still facing each other for a second, and then we were dancing. My ma says there is nothing better than dancing with someone who can dance well, and she is right.

After a while, I realized the people around us were clapping—they had stopped dancing just to watch us. It was the opposite of what we planned. We were supposed to be melting into the background, but something about the moment we were in made me feel like it was ours and it was worth it.

I glanced up at the clock. Midnight. Sylvia would be walking over to get Agapantha now.

"Go," I whispered to Stan as the music came to an end, and I gave him a push.

But as he left the room, the music stopped completely and Lord Portland-Prince stood at the top of the staircase to give a speech. The king and queen looked on as Agapantha stood next to them, desperately shaking her head at Sylvia on the stairs below her. Sylvia was scanning the room frantically, looking for some sort of answer, but there wasn't one. Six hundred people were staring at Agapantha. There was no escaping now.

Lord Portland-Prince thanked the king and queen for attending and the room politely applauded.

Sylvia saw me and pushed her way back through the crowd. "It's over, Myrtle. There's nothing to be done." She was almost hysterical.

I looked around for some sign of what to do next, trying to keep calm so my brain would work.

Then I saw it. One of the grand centerpieces, an enormous tower of champagne glasses stacked like a Christmas tree.

"Sylvia, look."

Her eyes followed mine and then she nodded. "See you outside." I watched her glance around and walk slowly to the table before she looked around once more, took a breath, and pushed it over.

The crash was louder than anything I could have anticipated. It sounded like a bomb. Glass flew everywhere and people screamed, jumping out of the way.

I turned and ran through the door Agapantha had pointed me toward. I climbed the stairs two at a time and opened the door to her room. It was empty. As I dragged the bag out from under her bed, she appeared, breathless. She peeled her clothes off as quickly as she could, and I helped her into her suit. While I shoved her Poseidon costume inside a bag, she ran and got Queenie's carry case. "You'll both look after her, won't you?"

"I promise."

The last thing was the tiara. She took it off carefully, wrapping it in a blanket and gingerly placing it in the bag. I tried not to think about how much money I would be carrying.

I handed over the bowler hat, and she pulled it down her head as far as possible.

"Ready?" I said.

And then Agapantha kissed me on the cheek. "Thank you for everything." She handed me an envelope. "It's the money for all your work. Myrtle, you really are magical." And then we opened the door and ran down the stairs and out through the kitchen to the stables, where Sylvia and Stan stood next to Spots. Agapantha put her foot in the stirrup and swung her leg over the horse. I handed her bag to her.

"Quick!" Sylvia seemed frantic. "Delphine is coming. She saw me."

"There's my father!" Agapantha sounded shrill with terror. Lord Portland-Prince was running out of the house dressed in full military uniform.

And then Delphine appeared.

"Sylvia! What is going on? Father will *kill* you when he finds out you're here."

I turned away from her and stepped into the shadows. If she saw me, she would tell the duchess and that would be it, the end of everything.

Lord Portland-Prince was bright red, his fists clenched and his eyes bulging.

"Stan, get on the horse. Now!" Sylvia screamed.

Lord Portland-Prince reached us. "Agapantha, get down immediately! I said *immediately*! Get off that horse, god-damn it!"

Stan tried to run to the horse, but Lord Portland-Prince grabbed him and pushed him up against a wall. "How dare you. Who are you? Kidnapping my daughter!" He looked like he was going to hurt him.

Sylvia darted toward the horse and Agapantha stretched her hand out; Sylvia hitched her dress up and swung into the saddle behind her. "I'll bring her back," Sylvia shouted to Stan.

"Stop!" bellowed Lord Portland-Prince.

But Agapantha kicked the horse, and it was off, Sylvia's rainbow streaming out behind them and round Hyde Park Corner. Lord Portland-Prince's eyes followed her, too shocked to move, and he loosened his grip on Stan. I held Queenie close, grabbed Stan's hand, and then we ran.

26

COMRADES IN ARMS

Sylvia

Agapantha gently kicked the horse and it started to canter. She was leaning low and whispering in her ear, as if convincing her to go on the mission with us. The horse started to pick up the pace, but I wasn't frightened. Agapantha's horsemanship was superb.

"We need to get to the river!" I yelled, holding on to Panth's waist as tightly as I could.

"I know!" she shouted in reply. She didn't look back, but I did. The twinkling lights of the party were already in the distance. My heart was racing. Lord and Lady Portland-Prince might easily send someone after us and would almost certainly call the police. I closed my eyes and willed Myrtle and Stan to be all right.

I should have been cold, but the pure exhilaration of it was making my whole body tingle with a kind of energy I'd never felt before. The horse was at a full gallop now. Agapantha really was an exceptional rider.

As we crossed London Bridge, with the Thames on either

side of us, it felt as if we were flying. Like we were riding Pegasus! Once we'd reached the other side, Agapantha stayed close to the river. The moon was still huge in the sky, and every so often the moonbeams would reflect off the water and catch us in a strobe of light. By rights, we should have been terrified—of the night and of all the unknown dangers of London and the river. But I didn't feel it. All I felt was the rhythm of the horse and the excitement of our mission. This was being a *true* comrade in arms, helping Agapantha escape and become who she actually wanted to be.

Agapantha pulled on the reins and whispered gently in the horse's ear, and she started to slow. "It shouldn't be too far now."

She no longer needed to shout. The only noise was the sound of the horse's hooves and the lapping of the river. I leaned my head against her back.

"Panth, I honestly think you are the bravest person. I don't even mean the bravest person I have ever met; I mean compared to really *everyone*. Robin Hood and Emmeline Pankhurst and Hercules."

"I don't feel that brave, really. I mean, I know Mummy and Daddy will be desperately cross. And Mummy will be sad about me not finishing the season after all her efforts with the themes and my ball and everything. But truly, Sylvia, I don't think I have the courage to stay here and . . . I don't know."

But she did know, and so did I. Stay and do the season and dance with all the boring boys and then marry one of them and have your picture in *Tatler* saying you looked quite the English rose.

"It's funny, you know," I said. "That's all Delphine wants. To get married, and jolly good for her, I say, but you know, sometimes I think there are more girls like us than we realize. Ones who just haven't got anyone to confide in. Who haven't got any friends to help them escape."

We rode the last part in silence. I had no idea what Agapantha was thinking, but her body felt tense and her head stayed perfectly upright, facing the road ahead. When the ship came into view, it was bigger than I expected, but then I suppose one needs a big ship to navigate whatever treacherous oceans lie between here and South America. I suddenly started thinking about sea monsters and shipwrecks and islands full of poisonous snakes.

"I think it was right you went to your ball as Poseidon. The master of the seven seas."

But Agapantha didn't respond. She brought the horse to a stop a little way from the ship. I swung off and looked up at her—a heroine setting off on an adventure.

"It's funny that you have to pretend to be someone else just to bally well get to be yourself."

Agapantha smiled and jumped down. "Thank you!" she said to the horse, and bowed to her slightly. "I just have to get there. Once I do I'll figure out the rest."

I smiled, and she held her hand out to shake mine, like gentlemen.

"Sylvia, you are a true, true friend. And tell Myrtle too. You are both really the only true human friends I have ever had. Look after Queenie, won't you?"

"I promise."

She hugged me very suddenly, very sharply, swung her bag over her shoulder, and then walked away. I watched her approach a man who must have been the captain of the expedition. I held my breath for her and didn't let it out until I saw her walk up the gangplank and onto the ship. Lady Agapantha Portland-Prince had done it. She had escaped.

And I had helped her.

The horse seemed to sense that the urgency had dissipated and lolloped along at a much more contented pace. I stroked her mane. "Come on, we still need to get home, Spots." I squeezed my legs, and she broke into a canter. Just as I started to feel the chill in the air, the first lighter blues of the sunrise started to edge onto the horizon. I was alone, riding astride, dressed in silks of ten different colors and cantering through London. I felt invincible, like I had grown up in one crystallized moment.

When I got to Green Park, the gate was still closed. I shut my eyes and spoke aloud: "If I am brave enough to jump the gate, everything will be quite all right. Better than all right. It will happen. All of it. Myrtle and I will succeed. Fashion designers, like Coco Chanel or Vionnet. But wilder and more daring and more *us*."

I leaned down and whispered, "Will you jump the gate with

me?" and stroked the horse's head. She neighed softly. I gave her a kick, and we were off. I didn't close my eyes; the moon and the sun were in the sky at the same time. I laughed out loud as we jumped.

I led the horse back on foot for the very last part of the journey. We crossed the edge of the park and walked back into St. James's Square together. Serendipity House was silent. There were no signs that anybody thought anything was amiss. But as I led the horse into the stables, there, in her dressing gown and slippers, her long hair braided in neat ribbons, was Delphine. She pressed her hands to her lips and then threw her arms around me.

"We must be very quiet," she whispered. "No one has noticed a thing. Lord Portland-Prince didn't know it was you she left with. I came home and have been waiting at my bedroom window for you ever since. Myrtle got back all right, I saw her. She crept in the servants' entrance."

I felt tears of relief welling up. Myrtle had made it. I had made it.

"I saw you jump the gate, Sylv—you looked *magnificent*. Like a fairy queen. Like an actual goddess."

We led the horse into the stables and unbridled her. We crept back inside and up the stairs and into my bedroom.

"You're absolutely filthy," Delphine tutted, but I could tell she was fearfully impressed.

I looked down at my dress. It was covered in mud that had sprayed onto it as we rode. But my headpiece and cape remained intact. I looked at myself in the mirror. Part Iris, goddess of the rainbow, part wild animal.

Delphine started to unbutton my dress. "Sylv, you might get in the most fearful trouble. You do know that, don't you? If anyone finds out that you even went to the ball . . . let alone . . . anything else."

I nodded. "I know, Delph."

She handed me my nightdress and a cloth for my face. "I'd never tell on you, Sylv. We are sisters, after all. And you made my ball dress, the thing that made me feel like everything would be all right. Ever since that moment at the ball, I have felt like I have become the person I always wanted to be. Like I'm going to get the life I always dreamed of having."

"The dress didn't do that, really, silly thing—*you* did."

Delphine shook her head.

"No, none of it would ever have happened without the dress you and Myrtle made. My magic dress."

"Did you see Lavinia Andrews this evening?" I snort-whispered. "She looked like a huge ball of purple cabbage with a giant fried egg sewn right onto her backside."

Delphine was not one to seem unkind, but her eyes twinkled a little.

"Go to bed, little Sylv. I am not even the least bit jealous that you are so beautiful and talented."

"Why?"

"Oh, I don't know. Because you're also stark raving mad. And my sister."

We climbed the stairs and slipped through the curtains and into my bed. It was pitch-black. We lay side by side, just like the night Delphine had cried until her eyes were raw, the night everything magical had started to happen.

I fell asleep so instantly and deeply that when the breakfast gong went, I was thoroughly discombobulated. I am not a character in a novel, so I did not need reassuring that it had not all been a dream, especially with Delphine snoring like a drunk giant in a fairy story. It did, however, feel thoroughly strange going about the morning as if everything were the same.

Delphine and I entered the breakfast room in a possibly *too* bright and breezy fashion. It is a good thing Delphine is not hoping to become an actress, or a spy of any sort. She mentioned, probably *seven* times, how very, very well she had slept. And that, in fact, she could not remember a night she had slept better or more deeply.

"Too divine!" Marmalade said. "Are you desperately in love with someone? I always slept so deeply when I was madly pashed up."

"Please, not at the breakfast table, for goodness' sake," Father barked over his porridge.

I had chosen to take the silent route to innocence, which also caused suspicion. "Sylvia dear, you haven't decided to grow wisdom teeth, have you?" Marmalade peered at me. "My brother did that at your age and he didn't speak at breakfast for three years."

I shook my head and then nodded. "Well, I'm sort of mulling it over—you know how these things are."

Marmalade seemed entirely satisfied by this answer and went back to reading her letters. "My cousin Emma is coming to London to buy a Labrador. Can you *really* not buy them in Paris?" She casually opened the newspaper and took a sip of tea. And then she sat bolt upright.

"Oh, girls, *do* look! It's Agapantha. She's on page two of the *Times*!"

Delphine was genuinely excited and jumped up to look at it. But an odd lump had started to form in my stomach and crawl its way up my throat.

"*Look* at her!" Marmalade looked shocked. "She is . . . stunning. That short hair. Listen!"

She tapped the table in excitement with her spoon and cleared her throat. "*Last night at Apsley House, the cream of the aristocracy gathered for the debutante ball of Lady Agapantha Portland-Prince, hosted by her uncle, the duke of Wellington. The theme of the evening was Mount Olympus, and saw a new wave of luxury couture created—*"

"What!" I jumped up and grabbed the paper out of Marmalade's hands. "*Lady Agapantha wore the most striking costume seen yet this season, the designer unknown at the time of going to press, and she had dramatically cut off all her hair."*

Delphine gasped.

"She does look quite spectacular." Marmalade was clearly impressed. "Agapantha, eh? What a dark horse. A beautifully avant-garde dark horse."

"Oh, for goodness' sake, let me see." Father swiped the paper out of my hands. He examined it and then turned the page. And then he sat down and went completely silent. He started to breathe in and out heavily. Delphine and I exchanged a look. He laid the paper down on the table on a new page, and there Myrtle and I were, right there in black and white. Both of us were midstride, staring up at the house, dazzled. Our masks by our side, our faces completely visible, blissfully unaware our photograph was being taken.

"Is . . . this . . . you?" Father asked in a voice I had never heard him use before.

Marmalade peered down and looked a little confused. "Good Lord . . . is that the maid?"

For a moment, a silence fell. We all stayed completely still, as if we were posing for a portrait. And then there was a knock at the door. Mrs. Piercy entered.

"Lord and Lady Portland-Prince, sir," she said to Father. But before we could arrange ourselves in any semblance of respectability and composure, they were very much in the room. Lord Portland-Prince did not go in for any introductions.

"Where is my daughter?"

"For God's sake, why on earth should I know where she is?" Fa shouted. He was still desperately confused, poor thing. "Can't you keep tabs on your own daughter?"

Delphine winced at the obvious misfire.

"My daughter has vanished. Vanished, I tell you!"

I looked down at my toast and honey and tried to appear nonchalant, as if the whole thing had nothing to do with me.

"This all seems rather dramatic." Marmalade sighed. "She's almost certainly eloped, dear Lady Portland-Prince. You know how girls love to elope. So romantic. So literary. I mean, could it be just a good old-fashioned dash to church?" She smiled a sort of you-know-how-trying-the-young-are smile. Lady Portland-Prince's mouth dropped open.

"How dare you?" She shook her head. "You have always been . . . scandalous."

Marmalade shrugged, but I could see a tiny hint of pride creeping toward the sides of her mouth.

Lord Portland-Prince had gone purple. And then all of a sudden he slammed his fist on the table and pointed at me.

"*You* are the girl from last night. My wife recognized you immediately! Where is my daughter? I say, where is my daughter?"

Everyone's eyes were suddenly on me. Delphine had started to weep, really quite loudly. I took a deep breath.

"Well . . ."

"Give me the address of where my daughter is hiding and with whom!"

"The thing is . . . I really can't."

Father cleared his throat. "Sylvia, if you know where this Panther girl is, you will tell Lord Portland-Prince this instant."

"All right, I will. I don't have an exact address, because . . . well . . . she's gone . . . to the Amazon on an expedition to find new species of animals."

It was quite apparent that this was not the answer that either Lord or Lady Portland-Prince—or anyone, really—had been expecting.

In the silence that followed, I tried to look demure and affect a sort of confused expression. But Marmalade had picked up the newspaper again with a keen eye. As her gaze swept over the page, her demeanor changed. She sat up very straight and crossed her arms.

"Where is my daughter? Where is she?" sobbed Lady Portland-Prince, sinking into a dining chair. "Where is my daughter?"

"More to the point," Marmalade said in an arch voice, "where is my tiara?"

27

BETRAYAL

Myrtle

Mrs. Piercy stared at the tiara. She didn't touch it; it was too priceless an object. Mr. Corbet opened the top drawer of my little chest under the window and took out the envelope of money Agapantha had given me. He opened it and showed it to Mrs. Piercy. She barely looked at it, like she feared she would be dirtied by association.

"I'll go to the duke presently," Mr. Corbet said, and put the envelope in his pocket. He picked the tiara up very cautiously and closed the door.

Mrs. Piercy suddenly had hold of both my shoulders. I bit my lip to stop myself gasping in pain. She shook me so violently my head hit the wall behind me. "They could hang you!"

She shook me again, this time even harder. "If someone put you up to it—your ma, or that boy who came here—if it was him, for the love of God, just tell Lord Cartwright, and he'll get the police. Myrtle—"

She dropped her arms to her sides, and I realized she wasn't furious, but scared. She was shaking her head, and her eyes were desperate. "If you confess now, it will go better for you, love. You probably don't understand how bad this could get. They still hang people for stealing food, never mind" — she dropped her voice to a whisper as if the word were more valuable somehow — "diamonds."

I reached down and took her hand in mine. She flinched at the forwardness but didn't pull away. I looked her straight in the eye.

"Mrs. Piercy, you have always been kind to me. I have broken the rules, I know that. But the money is payment for the costume I made for Lady Portland-Prince. I didn't steal it. And I was going to give the tiara back to . . ." I trailed off; it sounded so pathetic and ridiculous and untrue. Last night as I had crept back into the house, it had seemed too dangerous to go to Sylvia's room with the tiara and Queenie. How could I have been so foolish, and at the very last hurdle as well? I closed my eyes and willed my voice to stay even. "The tiara was just part of Lady Agapantha'a outfit. I know it looks as if I took it, but Mrs. Piercy, all I can do is promise you, on my father's name, that I have not stolen anything."

She observed me for a moment. "Oh, Myrtle, you stupid, stupid girl. If that is true, be brave and hold your head high, and God bless you. It surely isn't for me to pass judgment."

We walked in silence to Lord Cartwright's study. She was shaking slightly, more frightened than me. She knocked and he called us in. "Here she is, sir."

Lord Cartwright was sitting behind his desk. "Leave me

with the girl." I stood straight and looked right at him as Mrs. Piercy shut the door.

"My daughters have been naive. They were taken in by you. They do not realize how cruel and deceitful the world can be."

"I do not consider myself deceitful."

He seemed perturbed by my calm, as if he had been expecting a pathetic, crying weakling. "At the very least, you have tricked your way into my daughters' affections to climb your way up London society under false pretenses. You lied your way into a ball—"

"I did not. I was invited."

"You were not!" he thundered. "Lady Portland-Prince checked, and there was no one with your name on the list of invitees. You pretended to be someone else. That is fraud. And fraud is a crime."

I thought of Sylvia laughing and how sure she had been that no one would find out, "let alone care." But really what she meant was that *she* didn't.

Lord Cartwright took my silence as an admission of guilt.

"It is lucky that Lord and Lady Portland-Prince do not want a fuss. But their daughter is missing and no doubt you are to blame. Agapantha is apparently a sweet girl who would never have thought of such a thing on her own. And as for the theft of my wife's tiara, you should be grateful the police have not been called. Rest assured, I wanted them to be. The duchess is a more forgiving soul than I. Of course, you are sacked without pay or reference. The thought of someone like you befriending my daughter is disgusting to me. Now get out of my house."

Disgusting to me. I let the words permeate my body. I was disgusting to him. It seemed wrong to curtsy, so I didn't. I turned away and opened the door, just in time to catch sight of Sylvia running down the corridor.

The last time I had seen Sylvia she had been dressed as Iris and escaping into the night. She had seemed so brave and beautiful to me then, but now she didn't seem either of those things. She didn't even have the courage to face me. It was as if we were strangers, with nothing at all between us.

None of the other servants spoke to me as I climbed the stairs to the attic, but when I got there, Dot and Mary and Gladys were waiting. Gladys was sobbing so hard her breathing was jagged and gulping. Mary's arm was around her. Dot stepped forward and handed me a little cotton bag. "We all chipped in a bit. It ain't much, but it'll get you home at least."

She opened the door to my little room; it was completely bare again. They had packed my case and my sewing machine and perched on top of it was Queenie in her little travel box.

"There's some sandwiches in the suitcase," Gladys managed through sobs.

"We know you ain't no thief," Dot said matter-of-factly. "You're our friend. And I still think you're gonna be someone fancy, Myrtle."

"Thank you all, so much."

I picked up my things and tried to walk evenly, with purpose.

I could hear Stan at the warehouse: *She ain't your friend . . .*
It's always us who ends up getting it. He had been more right
than I could ever have known.

The hurt was seeping deeper and deeper inside of me, and
alongside it, shame. I had been useful to her. I had distracted
her and given her something to do. The House of Serendipity
was a game she had played for a bit. And I had believed it like
some stupid little sister. I had planned my life as if I could be
a fashion designer. As if I could change my destiny, when I of
all people knew that you can't control the fates. If that were
true, Pa wouldn't be dead and I would never have had to come
here at all.

Pa taught me to be proud, and I would leave here with my
head held high, whatever was being said about me. I should
have walked back down the servants' staircase, but I didn't. I
kept thinking of Sylvia turning and running from me. Stan had
been right—they were careless people who only thought about
themselves. It burned inside me. She could have defended me,
but she chose not to. She had never been my friend. I walked
down the main stairs and on toward the plush pink-and-red
walls of the east wing. I didn't knock on Lady Sylvia's door,
just walked straight in. She was sitting in her gondola and
turned around when she heard the door. I put Queenie gently
down, and she scrambled out of her box. Sylvia looked
frightened.

"Myrtle." Her voice was tiny. "I will . . . I will make sure
you get the money for . . . everything."

The insult of it, that she thought that was what I had come for, boiled up inside of me. "I don't want your money. All your money, all of this." I flung my hand over the room. "It all disgusts me. All of it. You swear things upon your honor as a lady, but that doesn't make you honorable. Nothing would make *you* honorable. You are a coward and a traitor."

Tears were running down my cheeks, but I didn't care. "You told me that nothing bad could happen to me because you were my friend and you would make sure of it. You're a liar, Sylvia. You didn't stand up for me." I almost screamed it at her, jagged and raw. "It was *you* who took the tiara, *you* who told Agapantha I was Lady Calypso. *You* who made me go to the ball. And you didn't stand up for me."

"I couldn't," she said. "I . . . I am already in so much trouble . . ."

"*You* are in trouble." I laughed. "Stan's right, people like you take what you want and don't care who you take it from."

"Myrtle, I'm . . ." She stood up in the gondola.

"Shut up. You are nothing to me. Comrade!" I spat the word out. "You will never have a true friend, because the only thing you care about is yourself."

I picked up my suitcase.

"Wait!" She moved to climb down the ladder. But in her rush the gondola tipped forward. I saw Sylvia try to regain her balance but fail. It was so quick that by the time I reached her, she had fallen all the way to the ground. I heard her head crack as it hit the floor. She lay completely silent and completely still, except for a trickle of blood leaking from her head.

"Help!" I screamed as loudly as I could, and pressed my hand against Sylvia's head to stop the blood. "Help me!"

Dot and Mary rushed in. "Go, Mary, go get help." And then Dot looked at me. "Myrtle, go now, before they see this. Get out and get away as fast as you can."

"I can't. I saw what happened. I—"

"Myrtle, they will blame you, whatever happened. This could make things even worse for you." She was crouching by Sylvia. "This is your last chance. Think of your ma, Myrtle. Go!"

"Will she be all right?"

But before Dot could answer, Mary appeared and shoved the suitcase into my hand. "You'll have to leave your machine. Gladys is waiting—she will make sure you get out. Run."

28

BATTLE SCARS

Sylvia

I felt underneath my pillow, found the tiny brass key, and opened the design book. I only allowed myself to look at it when I was quite alone. There was no one who could possibly understand what I was feeling, no one except perhaps Myrtle, and who knew where she was, or if she was even all right? It had been three weeks since my accident. I had tried to ask the maids when they came in with my trays, but they had looked at the floor, curtsied, and said, "I'm sure I don't know, ma'am," and then scuttled away. They could never say it, but I *felt* it. That they blamed me. They knew I should have done something to save her. And they were right. The shame of it weighed on me, and in my nightmares I would see Myrtle, waiting for me to help her again and again.

Seeing Myrtle's precise handwriting next to my designs — *Train in chiffon? Silk too light to hang like this* — made the ache all the worse. It wasn't loneliness as Marmalade thought, or my injury as Fa did. It was shame as sticky and black as treacle. It clung to everything now and stopped me being able to be me. Or at least who I used to be. It was impossible to explain, so I preferred to have no visitors and just sit hidden inside the curtains of the bed.

I heard the unmistakably slow and methodical steps of Miss Smurfett entering the room, and I threw the covers over my head. "Smurf, please do go away. I am simply not in the frame of mind for talking about Greek pots today."

There was a rustling as she quite ignored me and sat down on the armchair she had taken to reading to me in. "Indeed, Lady Sylvia, I suppose in one's life there is a *time* for Keats."

I threw the covers off. "Yes, jolly right. And it's not mid-afternoon."

Queenie scuttled herself up to the Smurf's chair and was promptly picked up and stroked like a cat. There was a knock at the door, and then Mrs. Piercy came in and put a tray of tea things on the bed. "I said I didn't want anything."

"The duchess said to bring the tray up just in case, Lady Sylvia." She curtsied before giving my scar a second look and leaving the room.

We sat together in silence for a while with just Queenie's purrs between us. "Miss Smurfett," I said finally.

"Yes, Lady Sylvia?"

"I want to be a better person. I feel as though the one I am is not at all the one I want to be."

Miss Smurfett took a cucumber sandwich and put it on her plate. "I have known you since infancy, Lady Sylvia, so I feel I can say with some degree of certainty that you of all people have the courage to become whoever and whatever you please."

"Do you really think so?"

"Indeed, I do." She bent over and opened her carpetbag. "And I was thinking, perhaps for a change, you might read me the newspaper today."

I groaned loudly, but the twinkle in her owlish eyes was brighter than ever as she passed me the *Times*. I opened it and looked down. Most of the page was covered by a picture of Agapantha. She looked exactly the same as she had the last time I had seen her, in her suit, except this time, the jungle was behind her and she was wearing a huge grin.

The spirit of Britain is alive and well and in the Amazon. Lady Agapantha Portland-Prince, at only seventeen, has intrepidly joined the Natural History Museum's summer expedition. She is the first woman to ever take such a role, which will involve a thousand-mile trek through uncharted jungle to document new species of animals.

Miss Smurfett poured me a cup of tea. "Do you know, I think that these are quite unprecedented times to be a young woman. If Lady Portland-Prince can decide who she wants to be and be it, I daresay you can too."

"You are a good egg, Miss Smurfett, even with the fractions and odes and tectonic plates and whatnot."

"Praise indeed," she said before the door swung open and

in spun Delphine. She was wearing a cream blouse with ruffles all over it and three strands of long pearls. Her hair was freshly waved, and she fizzed with confidence in a way I had never seen before. The new Delphine was what the papers called "a gal about town" and was thoroughly pleased with herself. Miss Smurfett bade us goodbye and Delphine got fully in the swing of things.

"I have the most delicious news." She opened up the bed-curtains fully and sunshine streamed in. She picked up both my hands in hers. "Bertie Foster came to tea." She let out an elated kind of yelp. "Yes, little Sylv, yes."

She was nodding as if I completely understood, when I understood nothing at all. "Yes, what?"

She threw her arms around me and kissed me on the cheek. "He asked to speak to me quite on my own, and then . . . oh, Sylv, it was so dreamy. The most delicious moment of my life."

"Having tea on your own with Bertie Foster was the most—"

"He proposed, Sylv! He said I was terribly pretty and most exciting. Can you believe it—*exciting*!"

I honestly could *not* believe it. I mean, it was frankly un-believable.

"What, you're going to marry Bertie Foster? *Marry?*"

"Well, that's the thing. I said no!"

"*What?* All you've been blathering on about your whole life is falling in love and getting married. I thought that was all you cared about."

"It *was*! And being proposed to was too, too divine. I simply *adored* it. And Bertie Foster is just the ticket, but really, little Sylv, I just live for the parties and the dresses and the gossip, and I simply can't bear to give it all up. Not yet, anyhow."

"Well, that is a bit contrary, I must say. To go and on and on about wanting someone to ask you to marry them and then refusing to when they do. We could have jolly well given up on this whole season before it even began."

She roared with laughter. "But it has been the dreamiest time of my life. And it was all you, Sylv. You and Myrtle. You made my dress, and that changed everything. *You* changed everything."

I leaned back on the pillow. Our success with Delphine's ball gown seemed terribly far away now, a very long-forgotten happiness.

"Oh, do try not to be so sad, little Sylv. You do look frightful, even without . . ."

"You can say it—my *scar*. I keep hearing people muttering about it, anyhow. It is as if I were a priceless painting that's been scratched and is now utterly worthless."

"*Priceless* is indeed *the* word for you, Sylv." She reached into her pocket and took out a letter and handed it to me. It had lots of stamps on it, from America. "I don't know anyone in America," I said.

"It's my official thank-you," she said. "For changing my life. I got a letter after my ball asking me who made my dress. I wasn't going to reply to it." She shrugged. "But then I changed my mind." She winked at me. "Well, I'm going to Ascot tomorrow. Marmalade is coming too. Must go and try my dress on. Don't tell Pa," she whispered, "but I do wish you and Myrtle were making it." She sashayed out and left me alone with the letter.

I opened it and read it. And then I read it again. This was it. My moment to become who I wanted to be. *What* I wanted to be. I flung the window open and the wind blew in. The last of the cherry blossoms danced around me as I looked out across London. Myrtle was out there somewhere. I just had to find her.

29

CHOICES

Myrtle

On the day I had left, I hadn't consciously gone to Stan's—I had gone home. It was as if my whole brain had switched off, but my heart had known how to get me there. I had walked for hours, all the way there. When I arrived, he made me a cup of tea and said I could stay for as long as I needed. We made a little bed for me in the corner of the workshop that we tidied away each morning. Stan said when his dad got back he would deal with him, but he hadn't yet.

I laid out the cutting table tools and got the mannequin with the suit we were adjusting for a lad getting married and then settled down to try and write to Ma. I picked up the pen and dipped it in the ink and stared down at the paper. But what could I say that she would understand? I needed to tell her that I had been sacked. That I had left Serendipity House in disgrace, that I was close to homeless, that I was ruined . . . that I was sorry. But I didn't even know if I was sorry. At night alone in my bed on the floor, surrounded by the rolls of fabric and cuttings, I held the key to the design book in my hand and lay there and let myself remember. Remember how magical it had all felt, and how for days I had woken up feeling like something special was happening, that I was making my own destiny. That *we* were. I let myself think about Sylvia, and a shudder ran over me. Whether or not she had believed in the House of Serendipity, *I* had. I had felt it when Delphine was announced at her ball and when Agapantha rode away into the night. I had felt it myself when I danced in my Hecate dress. I wanted to feel ashamed and wish it had never happened, but I couldn't—it was the most magical life had ever felt.

Stan burst into the shop just as I was opening the till. "Myrtle!" He kind of whooped to himself in delight and took his hat off. "You've really shown 'em." He laughed again. "Talk about beating them at their own game!"

"What are you blathering on about?" I could see he had something under his jacket. "What?"

He handed me a magazine. It was *Tatler*. And on the cover, with the light of the moon streaming in through the window, in floor-length black, was me. If someone calls your name, you don't think about how your face looks as you turn. My mouth was slightly open. I looked surprised and maybe curious, I don't know. Not how I had felt at the time. The cover said *The muse of the decade*. The dress looked more beautiful photographed than it had in real life.

"My dress. On the cover of a magazine." Whatever else had happened, this proved it. It couldn't all be forgotten; I would keep it always. The dress I had made was on the cover of a magazine.

"You. You're on the cover of a magazine." He was shouting it and laughing at the same time, shaking his head in disbelief.

We both peered down at the strange, grown-up, elegant me on the cover, and I suddenly felt shy.

"He took that picture without asking me." My cheeks were flushing.

"I would say I can't believe it," Stan said, "but I blinking well can."

The bell rang, and I turned the magazine over on the counter. I saw Stan's face glowering, and then I saw Sylvia. My stomach lurched and my heart started to beat hard in my chest. It was strange to think of how close we had been, seeing her standing there so formally. She was more conservatively dressed than usual, in a plain blue day dress and matching blue cloche hat. She didn't look like her; she looked like all the smart girls her age do at a party, conservative and demure. She stepped into the shop with a quietness I had never seen before, and behind her, dressed in red silk from head to toe, was the duchess. She looked so entirely out of place that people in the street were stopping to stare.

"Myrtle, first of all, I should like to say that my husband is truly sorry for being so desperately rude to you. As we have seen from wars and the general course of history, men often become most confused about what is what." I was too taken aback to speak. She reached into her pocket and produced an envelope that she handed to me. "Here is the money that you earned and so is rightfully yours. My husband also realized, after I instructed him to do so, that he has a keen interest in investing in your future. Mrs. Piercy tells me you would like to buy your mother a shop. Well, with what is in there and our best wishes, I very much hope you do so."

I stared at the envelope and all I could get out was "My ma."

The duchess flipped over the magazine on the counter. "Bit much to be knocked off being the beauty of the age by one's own maid, I must say. But I suppose these are the modern times they keep talking about." She turned around to leave and was confronted by the crowd who had gathered to watch her. "I'll wait for you at the car," she said to Sylvia, and strode out.

Sylvia and I were face-to-face. There was a part of me that was just elated to see her, alive and standing in front of me. Dot had written and told me she was going to be okay, but seeing her made it feel real. There was another part of me that wanted to run away. She had created everything that was wonderful in my life and everything that was terrible all at the same time. Seeing her felt like too much, as if my body was overwhelmed by it.

"You look well," I said finally. "I'm sorry that I made you fall."

Sylvia shook her head hurriedly. "You didn't. I made myself fall. Everything that happened . . . it was my fault. I am so sorry my father said those things to you, but I am much,

much more sorry that I didn't stand up for you when he did. I don't think I realized until that moment, when I was such a coward, what true courage is. You are so courageous, Myrtle. From the very first moment, you were so heroically brave and I was so perfectly stupid that I didn't even realize. I am truly ashamed, I am."

She didn't cry. I knew she wouldn't, because she wouldn't want it to take away from her apology. Even though I never thought someone like Sylvia would belong in this shop, I couldn't help feeling as if she did. She understood me, because she understood what mattered to me, how I thought, and how my brain worked. Ma and Pa weren't here, and even though it made no sense that Sylvia and I were connected, somehow, through the clothes and through everything that happened, we just were.

"Stan was right. You will never understand how it all felt from my side." And that was true, but there were parts of me that *only* she could understand too. We were intertwined but completely separate pieces of yarn.

"I see that now. I know I can't ever make up for it, but I want everyone to know how talented and special you are. And now maybe they will." She fished inside her pocket, took out an envelope, and held it out to me. It was addressed to her.

"What is it?" I looked at the rows and rows of American stamps.

"It's an invitation from Pinnacle Studios. From a director called Cal Logan. He saw the pictures of our dresses in *Queen* and *Tatler*. He wants you to go over there, to Hollywood. He wants you to design the costumes for his next film. It's called *California Waltz*."

My heart leaped out of my chest. I couldn't help it, even after all the false hopes, the dream was too strong inside me. "What do you mean, me?"

"Well, Lady Calypso Mortimer doesn't exactly have an address to correspond with. So it came to me." She tried to say it lightly, but she couldn't quite carry it off. "But I have written to him and told him that it isn't me whom he needs, but you. That you are the talent. *You* are the magician. *You* are the one who turns people's dreams into actual real-life things you can touch. I told him Myrtle Mathers is the greatest fashion designer the world has seen. I told him that because it's true, Myrtle. You will have your name on the credits at the end. And people all over the world will see it."

I imagined the letters of my name rearranging against a black screen: *Costume Design — Myrtle Mathers*. I imagined my mum's face. And then my dad's.

"You'll go, won't you?" she asked.

I turned around. Not to deliberately turn my back on Sylvia, or on Stan, for that matter. But because I wanted to look at the shop. Our shop. I still felt like it belonged to my family. I thought of all the memories that had been woven here. The people who should still be here and were not. I wondered what my dad would say. Hollywood. And our name: Mathers. And not just above a shop, but on the silver screen. I caught a glimpse of Stan. He looked proud as punch, like he was gonna burst with it.

"I *am* a good dressmaker. But I am not a good fashion designer. All those ideas—Poseidon, Iris, Hecate—they all came from you."

"Yes, but without you, they're just nursery school pictures. Myrtle, I am truly sorry. It was my fault. Every last single bit of it. The truth is I don't think I realized how possible it is to hurt a person until I hurt you."

She didn't say it in a gushing way, just very matter-of-factly. I realized that she looked more grown-up since I had last seen her. Her face seemed more striking than ever, despite the purple scar across her forehead. I had missed her. She made me feel like the world was a place full of fun and possibility and magic. Like together, *we* were magic.

I looked up at Sylvia and met her gaze dead-on. It was another risk, but wasn't everything in life? And on our own nothing had happened—it was when we were together that magic followed us.

"I will go, but only if you come with me. You are my friend. *We* are the House of Serendipity." I took my key to the design book out of my pocket. "It simply doesn't work without both of us."

Sylvia reached into her pocket and took out her key. As she did, a cherry blossom petal flew out and landed on my hand.

She rushed and flung her arms around me. "Then let's take our magic to Hollywood, together!"

ACKNOWLEDGMENTS

The first and biggest thank-you has to be to Julie Rosenberg at Razorbill and Sarah Stewart at Usborne. When we started working on this book together, none of us could have predicted what 2020 had in store. This has been an unprecedented year to be a teacher (or anything for that matter!), and I struggled at many points juggling remote and keyworker schooling with writing. Throughout everything, you were endlessly supportive, kind, and accommodating, and I really don't think I could have done it without you. You have both made this book infinitely better, and I am in awe of the way your brains work. Thank you!

In terms of research, I am incredibly grateful to the teams at both the London Library and the Victoria and Albert Museum study rooms. Thank you for helping answer my endless questions and for recommending books, pieces of art, and even fabric shops. The idea for this book came from Cecil Beaton's portrait of Nancy Beaton as a shooting star and a conversation with a librarian about its creation. A belated thank-you also to my father, who isn't here to receive it. Your love of Evelyn Waugh, Nancy Mitford, and P. G. Wodehouse via Just William certainly helped me arrive at Serendipity House.

Molly Ker Hawn, thank you endlessly for your direct, no-nonsense realness, and for supporting the idea for this book from the outset.

Always thanks to my coven: Alexie, Kate, Chrissy, Nell, Vicky, Yasmina, Laura, Ella, Lou, Anna, Lisa, Fiona, Angie, Tricia, and Cat.

And to early readers: Anya Sultan, Arianna Enserro, Holly Bourne, and Maartje Geussens.

And to late reader Rachel Smith, who very much got me through the COVID draft!

A massive thanks also to Lucy Elphinstone, who is always very supportive of my side hustle, and to all the staff at Francis Holland SW1, especially Robbie Ellen, Jay Deblue, Caroline Smith, and Irina Ramage (Irina, our form would literally fall apart if you were not there). I feel very blessed to work in such a brilliant, unique, and happy place.

Tom Ellen, thank you for declaring, "I know nothing about 1920s fashion, so you know—you're on your own for this one." I have missed your banter, copyediting skills, and complaining more than you will ever know. Truly, you're a good best friend to have.

Sandra Tweedie and Annabel Campbell, your dressmaking knowledge and insights have been invaluable.

Thanks to my mum, who over the years has been forced to read endless drafts of GCSE and A-level coursework, and now this book. You always had interesting things to say—thank you.

Also, to Mrs. Jackie Baker: guiding star and grammar guru.

Diana Battle, thank you for the cups of tea and time management.

And finally, Oliver . . . I almost didn't write this book because we were having too much fun. Even though you always suggest "adding time travel or aliens" when I am stuck, there is no one I laugh more with. Thank you.